Jessie Fothergill

Probation

A Novel: Vol. I.

Jessie Fothergill

Probation
A Novel: Vol. I.

ISBN/EAN: 9783337054038

Printed in Europe, USA, Canada, Australia, Japan

Cover: Foto ©Andreas Hilbeck / pixelio.de

More available books at **www.hansebooks.com**

PROBATION.

A Novel.

BY

THE AUTHOR OF 'THE FIRST VIOLIN.'

' Life let us cherish !'

IN THREE VOLUMES.
VOL. I.

LONDON:
RICHARD BENTLEY AND SON,
Publishers in Ordinary to Her Majesty the Queen.
1879.

PROBATION.

BOOK I.
PRIDE AND PLENTY.

CHAPTER I.

OF AN ABSENTEE EMPLOYER.

'The perfection of mechanism, human and metallic.'

YOU, at any rate, Lancashire reader, know this place; the large, somewhat low room; the long lines of looms.; the wheels, straps, and beams; the rows of standing workpeople, men, women, and children; the dimness of the dust-laden atmosphere. You know, too, the roar of noise—how deafening, stunning, and overwhelming it is to the stranger who may happen casually to encounter it, yet how easily those in the habit of working in it can make themselves intelligible to one another. You know all this, and your accustomed eye recognises at once one division of the 'weaving shed' of a large cotton factory; which forms, with its perfect mechanism, the 'metallic and the human :' a most wonderful sight to any eyes but the too careless or the too accustomed.

There is an air of calm, leisurely ease about the process which might be apt to lead the uninitiated astray, and make him suppose that not so much accuracy of eye, delicacy of manipulation, sensitiveness of touch, was required as is really the case. Which are the most alive—the girls in the cotton dresses, and the men in their fustian clothes, who move lightly to and fro, adjusting their work, keeping watch and ward over the flying shuttle; or that flying shuttle itself, which seems instinct with vitality, darting with vivid, almost oppressive, regularity of activity backwards and forwards—indulging sometimes in a malicious vagary, worthy of a human being, such as flying suddenly out from its groove, and perhaps striking its human fellow-worker a sharp blow on the forehead, or in the eye? It would be difficult to say—the definition at the head of the chapter forms also the best description of the whole—'the perfection of mechanism, human and metallic.'

It was during the afternoon hours of work; the day's labour was drawing to a close; the great ceaseless roar and buzz and rush seemed to grow rhythmic, harmonious in its monotonous continuity—through the thick-ribbed panes •of glass, distorted yellow sunbeams came streaming, golden, hazy, smoky, dusty, striking here and there upon the face of some laughing or languid girl; here into the eyes of some lad—an imp of mischief — or a youth of thoughtful and serious aspect.

1—2

That was the head overlooker who came in, looked round, stopped the loom of one of the said laughing girls, fingered the cloth, remarked warningly, 'Now, Sarah Alice! this won't do! You must look out, or there'll be some mischief;' then passed on his round, stopping more looms; examining more cloth, and then went out of the room altogether.

A steady progression, for a time, of the rhythmic toil, till the same door was again opened, and a young man, who also appeared to be a person of some authority, stepped in, and paused, note-book and pencil in hand. This was the second over-looker, a person who of necessity must possess considerable intelligence, being generally, as in this case, a working man, born and bred, some discrimination and tact also, since he fulfilled the duties, in some measure, both of a workman and a superior. In addition to his position as over-looker, he also performed the functions of what is known in factory parlance as 'head cut-looker;' and a cut-looker is a man who examines each piece or 'cut' of cloth after it leaves the loom ; notes the flaws, and deducts from the wages of the weaver in compensation for the same. Perhaps this 'cut-looking' and over-looking may be like criticising—they may have a tendency to produce a turn of mind sceptical as to the merits of the work with which the cut-looker, or the critic, has to do. Incessant flaws, 'scamped' work, broken threads, ill-joined ends, an uneven weft, a rough warp—the parallel is certainly a striking one ; and a long career of cut-looking, to say nothing of criticising, may tend to make the temper quick, and the tone just a little imperious.

The individual whose occupation was something like criticism, was a tall young man, dressed in grey clothes, which looked in some way cleaner, or better, or different from the clothes of the others, and a white linen jacket, which gave a cool and airy look to the whole costume, and was far from un-becoming to the spare, yet very strong, well-built figure, and to the dark, handsome, sharply-cut face belonging to it.

A right workmanlike figure. There was power and capacity—skilled power and capacity, too, in the supple, lissome figure, in the brown hands, long and slim, yet strong and muscular, which looked as if they were well-accustomed to do fine work, and to do it well. The loose linen jacket was by no means new, though clean; it bore here and there traces of having been mended, and sat in the easy creases and folds of a much-worn old friend, from whose shape no washing and starching can quite banish the accustomed outline, given by the wearer's form. Above the collar of this jacket was a narrow line of grey waistcoat; then a white collar, and a narrow black tie. The whole costume was as pleasant and as becoming to look at, as it was practical, fit, and workmanlike.

The face was rather thin and rather square; the complexion pale. The eyes were very dark and very steady—at the moment very quiet, though with a touch of defiance in them which was habitual; the forehead broad and thoughtful—the level eyebrows had a trick of contracting sharply, which took away from the calmness which might have seemed at first the dominant characteristic of the ample brow. The nose was rather long and sharp—the mouth firm, and a little cross : the lips looked as if they would more readily tighten in irritation at the stupidity of others, than part in wonder or amaze at their cleverness—and their expression did not belie the truth. The whole face was more clearly cut, more decided in feature, more distinct in expression than the faces of many—nay, of most of his class in the same place. Perhaps it answered to a clearer mental outline—was the distinct objective side of a well-defined subjectivity. Be that as it may, the figure was a manly and a good one—the face no less so.

This young man, holding his pencil suspended over his note-book, looked reflectively around the room, standing erect, though the wall was just behind him to lean upon. Walls to lean upon, moral or material, are irresistible to some people. His eyes fell upon the different workers as they moved hither and thither, adjusting their work, or stepping from one loom to another. Those eyes presently fell upon a young woman who was standing at the far-end of the room, and whose face happened to be turned towards him. Her glance met his : they nodded and smiled to one another, and his smile flashed across his dark face with an effect which the smiles of fair faces and light eyes can never have.

This young man's name was Myles Heywood, and the scene of his labours was the factory of Sebastian Mallory, the largest mill and property owner but one in the town of Thanshope, in Lancashire. He was, then, clever, honest, proud to excess, and self-opinionated, though few people could help liking him, even when his opinions and prejudices, with both of which articles he was well-provided, might rub against theirs. One thing deserves recording of him, which alone would have shown him to be somewhat aloof from his fellow-workmen—he had no nick-name; and in that district, where often a man's real name was quite hidden under a cloud of by-names and nicknames, this was at least peculiar.

Myles Heywood, after spending a few mo-ments looking down the shed, through the mist of cotton fluff which made the air dim and the lungs irritable, turned and went into a neighbouring room, where they were twisting—a monotonous task—the rapid twisting together of the ends of cotton of two warps, paid for at the rate of threepence per thousand ends—a fact which had caused our critic in the linen jacket much thought at different times.

Out of this twisting-room into a large square yard or court, with the engine-house and its neighbouring boilers on one side;

offices on another, and the great wall of the mill on the third. On the fourth, a blank wall and huge gates, at present standing open, and affording a glimpse into the dingy street.

The engineer, this warm August afternoon, was standing in the full glow of the furnace : his face was black, and shone as if recently it had been anointed with oil. His arms were bare and sinewy, and they were black too. His shirt, whatever its original hue, was black now, and his other garments, reduced to as scanty a quantity as was compatible with decency, were black also with oil, and grease, and coal-dust. He paused to mop away a swarthy perspiration with a dingy-looking handkerchief, as Myles went by, looking clean and cool, and aggravatingly comfortable.

'Hey, Myles, lad, what time dost make it ? I'm too hot to get my watch.'

'Ten to six,' said Myles, looking at his watch.

'The Lord be praised !' responded the engineer piously, 'and send us a speedy deliverance. It's as hot as hell here of a summer afternoon, and no jokin'. Hast had thi' baggin ?'*

'I don't take baggin,' said Myles, a little contemptuously, as he took his way to the office, where he found a man and a boy behind a desk, on which was a heap of gold, silver, and copper coins, and a number of books and papers. It was Friday afternoon —pay-day.

'Oh, you're there, Myles,' said the man. 'You may take your wages now, if you like.'

'All right !' said Myles, picking up two sovereigns from the heap of gold, and slipping them into his pocket. Then he twisted himself over the counter and seated himself on a high stool beside the desk.

'By your leave, I'll just wait here till my lass comes, and then we'll go home together.'

Wilson, the head-overlooker and cashier,

---

* 'Baggin' is not only lunch, but any accidental meal coming between two regular ones.

assented. Myles folded his arms before him and began to whistle a tune to himself. It was the tune of the song, ' Life let us cherish!' and when Myles had nothing else to do, he generally did whistle it—unthinkingly, almost unconsciously. While he whistled he looked through the dingy panes of a small window upon a prospect as dingy as the panes.

There was nothing but a short patch of grey-looking street, and over the way the multitudinous windows of a great foundry, from the back premises of which came loud, sonorous clangs, as of metal striking against metal—a maddening and a deafening sound to ears unused to it, but which, from long habit, failed to disturb the workers in ' Mallory's Factory.' It had become, not exactly inaudible to them, but part of the day's features—as clouds, or wind, or rain. They would, to use a Hibernicism, only have noticed it if it had left off.

It still wanted some eight or nine minutes

to the time when the bell would ring for 'knocking off' work, and that interval was used by those present to discuss with their tongues that with which their heads happened to be concerned, for the truth is, that out of the emptiness of the head, much oftener than out of the fulness of the heart, does the mouth speak.

'Hast heerd news, Myles?' inquired the lad.

The whistle ceased for a moment.

' What news?'

' We have heard say,' said the other man, ' as how he's coming home.'

' Who?'

Wilson pointed northwards, over his shoulder, with his thumb.

'Oh, him!' said Myles, with again the touch of contempt which came a little too often to his voice. And he shrugged his shoulders—another gesture betraying his unlikeness in temper and temperament to those with whom he was surrounded.

' Ay, him!'

' Is it true ?' inquired Heywood.

' Don't know.   I've only heard say so.'

' *Who* said so ?'

' Why, I believe it were one of the men from the stables at Mrs. Mallory's.'

' Servants' gossip !' said Myles trenchantly, unsuccessfully trying to turn up his nose. ' Never believe what they say.   Flunkeys by trade, and liars by nature, the whole lot of 'em, or they wouldn't be where they are.'

' I'm none so keen about believing every-thing that any one says to me,' said Wilson, with a slightly offended air, ' but this seems to me so uncommonly probable, with things in the state that they are.   Why shouldn't he come back ?'

' Ay, why shouldn't he ?' echoed Ben, the office boy, feeling a dawning sense of coming pleasure in the idea of having given Myles a poser.

' Why shouldn't he ?' began Myles.

' That makes three times as it's been said,' observed Ben, with an intelligent smile. ' Well ?'

'Young one, keep your fingers out of the pie!' said Myles, 'and answer me this—why should he?'

Crestfallen silence on the part of Wilson and Ben, till the former began, rather feebly:

'Well, he's been abroad for years and years, and when he's a fine property like this, a-waiting for him to step into, as it were, and a fine house, and a fine mother——'

'Ha, ha!' said Myles, and his laugh was by no means one of unsophisticated enjoyment.

'And with things in the state that they are,' Wilson again repeated, as if much impressed with that state. 'With these Yankees and Southerners at it like cat and dog, and cotton going up, and no prospect of any end to it yet. Mr. Sutcliffe said to me, he says, "Wilson, we don't know what's before us yet. If I'm not much mistaken," he says, "there'll be a famine in the land before this time next year." And I say, if a master

shouldn't come home under those circumstances, when should he?'

'Should! Ought!' repeated Heywood, in
sarcastic tones; his scornful smile lighting
his face, and gleaming in his eyes. 'What's
that to do with it? I'll tell you why he
couldn't, and shouldn't, and won't come.'

The others settled themselves more attentively in their positions to hear the riddle
answered.

'Because he's proud and lazy, and likes
amusing himself better than working,' said
Myles, with a strong flavour of contempt and
dislike in his voice. 'Because the money's
there, and let who may have made it, choose
how they've sweated for it, it's got into his
hands, whether he deserves it or not, and it's
his to do as he likes with—so he does what
he likes with it. He's got such a manager
as there isn't another like him in Lancashire.
Mr. Sutcliffe can do anything; it's he that
has slaved and made this business what it is
—the biggest in Thanshope, next to Spence-

ley's. He's got this manager, and if he chooses to think that he hasn't got a duty in this mortal world, except to muddle his head with foreign politics, as I hear he does, and amuse himself by dancing attendance on a lot of fine ladies, and stroll about foreign countries, and stare himself blind up at pictures as big as the side of a house, and as black as my hat, and figures of men and women without any clothes on——'

'Lord!' said Ben, awestruck and shocked.

'And go rambling about, admiring scenery, and wondering what to do with himself next —well, what is it to us?'

As Wilson and Ben really did not see what it was to them, but had an uncomfortable sensation that their hitherto revered and honoured Mr. Sutcliffe was in some way a wronged and slighted individual, and that they ought to feel it all to be a great deal to them, and a subject of soreness and offence, they waited humbly for the keynote, nodding their heads, and trying to look wise.

'It's true,' went on Myles, more warmly—
'it's true, he's got this big business here,
which makes his money, and hundreds of
hands who work for him, and who are, so to
speak, under his care; and it's true that
some people—old-fashioned idiots, of course
—might think that a big property has its
duties as well as its pleasures, and that a
capitalist has, or ought to have, something
else to do than take and spend his money,
and never inquire how he got it, nor what
state the machine is in that made it for him;
but what is that to us? If we're going to
have a famine in the land, it would be unpleasant for a person not accustomed to this
kind of thing—all the more reason for him to
keep away. My lord likes the company of
lords and ladies, and he thinks Thanshope is
only fit for tradespeople.'

'I bet he's ne'er seen nowt finer nor the
new town-hall, choose where he may have
been !' said Ben aggressively.

'And,' went on Myles, whose mouth had

grown very cross indeed, and whose eyebrows met in a straight line across his frowning brow, ' he's a *Tory*—a Tory ; if I'd said that at first, I shouldn't have needed to say all the rest. A Tory, in these times, and in Thanshope !'

Wilson and Ben laughed, but not quite a whole-hearted laugh. A Tory—every species of Conservative—was a poor thing, was the general Thanshope opinion, but they had always thought of Tories more as harmless old women, or vulgar ' risen ' men, like Mr. Spenceley, than as anything so actively mischievous and to be eschewed as their absentee employer, Sebastian Mallory.

' He's ashamed of the place, and the people, and the business that has made him what he is. And that's why he won't come back.'

' I say, Myles, who told you all this ?' inquired Wilson deferentially.

' That I'm not at liberty to say ; but not one of the men from the stables, old lad,' said

Myles. 'But my authority is a good one, and it's what I've suspected for years. I've heard of his doings. He goes about with parsons. He's trying all he can to shake himself free of trade. He'll try to do it by marrying a lord's daughter—that's what these shoddy Conservatives always do—she'll spend his money for him, and if he says anything, she'll tell him it smells of cotton, and she wants to get rid of it.'

'Nay, nay, now!' interrupted Ben, with feeling.

'But she will,' said Myles, looking as angry as if the fair and contemptuous aristocrat stood in person before them. 'I know. Don't we all know what happened to Jack Brierley's lad, and how——'

Clang, clang, clang! went the great bell in the courtyard. It was two minutes past six. Wilson raised himself rapidly from his recumbent attitude, and began to turn over his papers, calling Ben to his side to help him. The discussion as to the merits or demerits of Sebastian Mallory, who certainly formed a striking instance of the theory that *les absents ont toujours tort*, was over; soon the office was filled with a pushing, elbowing crowd, waiting more or less impatiently to receive the hire of their week's labour.

Myles sat upon his high stool in the background, and watched, while Wilson and his assistant paid out the wages. It was rather a dingy-looking crowd that he saw, and was apparent to nose, as well as to eye, by the unmistakable odour of oil and fluff which emanated from it. Bare-armed girls with long, greasy pinafores, loud voices, and ungainly gestures, elbowing their way through the lads, and exchanging with them chaff of the roughest description. Small, pale, stunted-looking men; sometimes downright hideously ugly and mean-looking, or again, only sallow, pale, and subdued by a sedentary occupation, with here and there a tremendous, massive brow; here and there a pair of eyes so deep and glowing as to cause a shock and thrill to one who encountered them; here a mouth of poetical delicacy and sensitiveness; there a jaw so strong and heavy that, comparing it with the eyes, brows, and mouths before spoken of, one no longer felt cause for surprise in hearing such aphorisms as 'Manchester rules England,' 'What Lancashire thinks to-day, England thinks to-morrow.' It was, taken all in all, an ugly crowd, but in its way a commanding one. It might have moved the soul of a 'Corn-Law Rhymer,' a Gerald Massey, a 'Lancashire Lad;' it would probably have been repulsive to more refined bards and writers, and the poet of the brush and canvas would have found absolutely nothing here with which to gladden his eye.

Myles, a striking exception to almost every one of the men in point of good looks and fine physical development, if not in point of intelligent expression, sat upon his stool; and his monotonous whistle continued, as he scanned the faces, and returned a nod here and there. Many a girl looked at·him, and smiled her brightest as she caught his grave eyes.

He was not quite like the other work-men, in more things than beauty, and a somewhat higher position, and none knew that better than the workwomen. The smiles and amiable looks provoked little answer. Myles was not rude to girls; he never chaffed them in the rough manner of some of his fellow-workmen; but, on the other hand, he very seldom took any notice of them at all, having very little to say to any young woman out of his own family.

They passed before him in varied array; ugly, and pretty, and mediocre; fair girls and dark girls, stout girls and thin ones, tall and short, stupid and intelligent-looking. Here and there a pale, pensive face, with a head of flaxen hair, and long, delicate, Madonna-like features; now a brunette, with high com-plexion, and flashing black eyes, that showed the brighter under the thick white powdering of cotton fluff with which her head was covered; piquante and placid, merry and melancholy; but not for one in all the crowd did his cheek flush in the least, not once did the calm indifference in his eyes change, nor did his low, careless whistle cease for an instant. He stared over or between their heads, or—which was the most irritating of all—right at them, without once noticing them, until a girl, somewhat taller than the majority of her companions, came in, and stood waiting with a group of others near the door, until her turn should come to go up for her wages.

Then Myles stopped whistling, and got off his stool, remarking, half to himself, 'There's Mary, at last!' and applied to Wilson for the sum of eighteen shillings, that being the amount of his sister's wages. He received the money, and made his way through the crowd towards the door.

'Eh, Myles, art there?' said the young woman. 'Wait of me a minute, while I get my wages.'

'They're here,' said he, putting the money into her hand. 'So come along, lass! Let's get out of this shop.'

They passed out at the door, and walked together down the sloping street—a tall and well-looking pair. It was very seldom, indeed, that Myles Heywood and his sister' Mary failed to walk home from their work together.

CHAPTER II.

'And I will say to my soul, Soul, thou hast much goods laid up for many years; take thine ease, eat, drink, and be merry.'

IT was August of the year 1861—the year succeeding that which might almost be called the apotheosis of the cotton trade. The goods of Lancashire were piled in every port; her merchants were a byword for riches and prosperity. 'Cotton lords'—the aristocracy of the land—that grimy, smutty, dingy, golden land, whose sceptre was swayed by King Cotton.

Day after day the goodly ships had borne

their load across the Atlantic, from New Or-
leans and the other cotton ports ; day after
day those Liverpool cotton lords had received
that load upon their docks, and those Manchester cotton lords had bartered with them
and bought it ; and it had been borne slowly
along, piled up on great lurries, or it had been
whirled along the iron road, and unloaded,
and carried to a thousand factories in Manchester, and Bolton, and Oldham—the giant
consumers ; in Rochdale, and Bury, and
Burnley ; Blackburn, and Wigan, and
Ashton, and Stockport ; to the great,
young, growing towns ; to strange moorland
villages, younger sisters of the towns ; and
there, thickset spikes had whirled it about,
and combs had smoothed it out; revolving
spindles had spun it into the thickest or the
most fairy threads ; rows and rows of shining
looms had received it, and woven it into every
conceivable variety of texture and colour, and
breadth and length, and pattern. Skilled
workmen and workwomen, deft-handed, lis-

some, soft-fingered craftsmen and crafts-
women had stood by their wooden and
metal fellow-workers, and fed their untiring
jaws; then it had gone to the white-looking
warehouses, to be piled in great masses, like
little mountains for height and solidity, and
from thence removed to ships again, and borne
over the seas to India, and China, and America, and to every town in Europe where
men and women needed clothing and had
money to buy it.

The glory of King Cotton at this period
of his reign, and the splendour of him, cannot be better summed up than in the graphic
words of one who has thought and written
on that great subject:

'The dreary totals which Mr. Gladstone's
eloquence illuminates, and the rolling nume-
rals of the National Debt, become almost
insignificant beside the figures which this
statement (the statistics of the cotton
trade) involves. Arithmetic itself grows
dizzy as it approaches the returns of the

cotton trade for 1860. One hundred years back, and the cotton manufactures of England had been valued at £200,000 a year. Had not French, American and Russian wars—had not railways and telegraphs, had their part and lot in this century, surely it would be known as the Cotton Age. This year, 1860, was the *annus mirabilis* of King Cotton. In this year his dependents were most numerous, and his throne most wide. There was no Daniel at hand to interpret to him the handwriting on the wall, which within twelve months should be read by all who ran, in letters of blood. What cared he? An argosy of ships bore him across every sea and into every port. He listened to the humming of his spindles and to the rattle of his looms; he drank of the fulness of his power and was satisfied, for he was great— yes, very great. . . . The total value of their (the manufacturers') exports for the year, amounted to £52,012,380. If figures can ever be magnificent—if naked totals

ever reach to the sublime—surely the British
cotton trade for the year 1860 claims our
admiration. Its production for this single
year equalled in value £76,012,380, or nearly
six millions more than the gross revenue of
the kingdom for the same period.'

Surely the land which was the chief home
of this monster trade deserved the title of
'The Land of Plenty,' and such it was—'a
goodly land,' in fact, if not in outward show,
'a land flowing with milk and honey,' or at
least their modern English equivalents—a
land where wealth was profuse—where masters and men vied with each other in pride of
bearing and dogged independence of spirit.
Such was that rough, dark land at the end of
1860; such it was still at the end of August,
1861; what it was in August, 1862, only
those know who dwelt in it, and saw its
thousands of perishing children, and noted
their stoic endurance of their sufferings.

Even now, even in this month of August,
1861, rumours were gaining ground that the

war in America would not soon be over. The price of cotton was beginning to go up; the days were hastening towards that month of October when prices sprang up, mounting daily higher and higher, and factories began to close—not in ones and twos as heretofore, not to run short time, or half time, or even quarter time, but to close bodily, in dozens and scores, with no prospect of their opening again for an indefinite period of want and woe. It was a vast, dark, pitiless cloud, that which was even now rolling up from the West, bearing in its huge womb lamentation, and mourning, and woe.

But still Lancashire was the land of plenty and of hospitality; still her generous fires burnt merrily upon her ample hearths, making the stranger forget her murky skies, and the smoke-dimmed countenance of her landscapes. Her workpeople still got the largest wages, her masters still made the greatest fortunes of any masters and work-people, taken collectively, in England; and

nothing was said about the over-production
of the last plethoric year, nor of the
piled-up goods in the overstocked warehouses.

CHAPTER III.

RIFTS WITHIN THE LUTE.

THE brother and sister walked together down the sloping street already mentioned, and which was, as usual at that time, full of workpeople, streaming out of the numberless factories which formed the staple of Thanshope buildings. Arms were swinging, and clogs were clattering; tongues were wagging furiously in the reaction of the release from work, and the inhalation of the air, which though close and thunderous, was yet fresher than that in the great hot factories.

Thanshope was built on a situation with considerable claims to natural beauty, and there were days, even now, when it looked beautiful. Its streets all climbed up and down steep hills. Whenever the day or the smoke was clear enough, hills might be seen surrounding it on all sides in the distance, except to the south, where Manchester lay.

There was a river—the river Thanse—running through the town, which unfortunate stream formed a fertile source of bickering and heart-burning amongst the members of the town council, the medical men, and the people who write to the newspapers: one party of them contended that there was nothing the matter with the river Thanse, it was a good and wholesome stream, which purified the town; while the other party said that it and its unspeakable uncleanness were at the root of all the ills that Thanshope flesh suffered from.

Altogether, the verdict of a stranger would most likely have been that Thanshope was a

dim, unlovely, smoky place, in which no one
would choose to live whose business did not
oblige him to do so—a place where substantial dirt was the co-operator of substantial
prosperity, where grime and plenty went
hand in hand.

Yet there were people who loved this dirty
town, and who lived contented lives in it :
people not belonging to the great swarm of
workers who were obliged to live there, and
who, perhaps, thought more about the rate
of wages than about the æsthetic condition of
their surroundings.

Myles and Mary Heywood, having come
to the end of the sloping street, turned a
corner to the left, and soon found themselves
in another street, quieter, wider, with terraces
of small houses on either side, whose mono-
tony was diversified by various chapels, meet-
ing-houses, and schools. Uphill for a short
distance, till the street grew wider and the
houses better, and Myles and Mary, turning
down a side street to the right, emerged upon

one side of a wide, open, square space, called Townfield, or the Townfield, and elevated so high that the rest of the town lay below them as in a basin. All along that side of the Townfield where they stood, was a row of neat, small houses, each exactly like all the others; the only room for the individuality of the owners making itself apparent, being in the arrangement of the little strip of garden spreading before each.

Half the Townfield had been cut off, a couple of years ago, to furnish a small park or pleasure-ground; but looking across the open space to the north-west, they could see the old part of the town in its hollow; the old church of the parish on ground almost as high as the Townfield itself; the gilded spire of the town-hall rising ambitiously from the hollow (it chimed a quarter after six with mellow tone as they stood there), and all the other churches and chapels, and public buildings strewn here and there about the town. A great cloud of smoke came up and dimmed

the air ; on every side was a fringe of long
chimneys ; different big factories were familiar
features in the landscape, and formed landmarks to Mary and her brother—had formed
landmarks to them from infancy.

Away to the north-west were undulating
lines of blue, lofty moors. They were part
of Blackrigg—that mighty joint of England's
irregular spine. It was not exactly an en-
livening prospect, but it had certain beauties of
its own ; and at least this town, full of rough,
busy toilers, had a fitting and harmonious
frame in that semicircle of bleak and treeless
moors.

Mary and Myles went up one of the strips
of garden about the middle of the terrace,
and opened the door of the house.

'Pah ! how hot and close it feels !' said
Myles, as they closed themselves in. 'Now
I wonder how that lad is !'

They went along a little passage, to the
left of which was the 'parlour,' arranged in

the approved style of such parlours, with a
brilliant, large-patterned carpet in red, yellow,
and blue; bright green merino curtains, a
' drawing-room suite' in rosewood and crimson
rep, a pink cloth upon the centre-table, upon
which were negligently arranged albums,
Sunday books, paper mats, and a glass shade,
under which reposed waxen apples and grapes
of a corpulent description. On the mantelpiece, two green glass vases, and a china
greyhound of an unknown variety, more
frilled paper mats, and little piles of spar and
crystal. On the walls, photographs and a
rich collection of framed funeral cards, together with the *chef-d'œuvre* of the whole
establishment—a work of art which Mary
regarded with feelings little short of venera-
tion—' Joseph sold by his Brethren,' executed
in Berlin wools, the merchants all squinting
frightfully, and Joseph with a salmon-
coloured back and a decidedly ruddy countenance, though one not of such remarkable

beauty as quite to account for his subsequent adventures.

Past the door leading into this epitome of art and beauty went these young people, into the kitchen, which was of course the general living-room of the family. Upon a couch beneath the window, with the crinkling of the cinders and the ticking of the clock for his only companions, lay the failure of his family—a cripple lad of eighteen.

'Well, Ned, lad, how dost find thyself?' asked Myles, going in.

'I find myself as usual—wishing I was dead,' was the encouraging reply, as the lad turned a pale and sallow face, not without considerable beauty of feature, but stamped with a look of ill-health, pain, and something deeper and more sorrowful than either, towards the strong, handsome brother who stooped over him.

'Nay, come! Not quite so bad as that,' said Myles, smoothing Edmund's hair from his hot forehead, and seating himself beside the couch. He looked into his cripple brother's eyes with a glance so full of life, and hope, and strong, protecting kindness. and withal so contagious a smile, that an answering, if a reluctant one, was wrung from the lad's dull eyes and down-drawn mouth.

'I'm that thirsty!' he said. 'Molly, do get the tea ready.'

'I'm shappin' (shaping) to't now, lad,' she returned. hanging up her cotton kerchief and poking the fire to settle the kettle upon it.

'And you read a bit, Myles, wilta?' pursued Edmund. 'Mother won't be home for half an hour, and I could like to know how yon Lady Angiolina got on at the castle.'

Myles took up a book from a table and began to read aloud :

'"As the groom of the chambers announced the Lady Angiolina Fitzmaurice, every eye turned towards her. She advanced with the step of a queen. Her trailing robe of black velvet set off her superb beauty to the utmost advantage," and so forth.

Edmund listened with face intent and a pleased half smile upon his lips. Mary moved noiselessly about, getting the tea-cups out of the cupboard and setting them on the tray with gingerly hand, so as not to disturb the literary party in the window.

The reading was continued only for the space of some quarter of an hour. The story was a novel of 'high life.' No agent in it was of lower rank than a baronet; no menial less distinguished than a groom of the chambers or a major-domo was permitted to appear in its truly select and exclusive pages: the action took place in Mayfair, in Belgravia, and in the ancestral halls of dukes and earls. Manchester was alluded to by the refined author much as if it had been of about equal importance with Timbuctoo; the whole a very tawdry tinsel, pasted together in a very poor, second-rate manner.

Myles read on and Edmund listened. Perhaps he was aware that the story was rubbish, but it took him into a world which by contrast with his own was beautiful: it spoke of something else than the Townfield as a pleasure-ground, grey factories, smoke and chimneys by way of a prospect. It pointed out another sort of existence than that led by him and his.

Edmund had an intensely poetic temperament. Poetry of some sort, in real life, or in books, he must have or die. It was not forthcoming in real life: Myles never read novels for his own pleasure, therefore Edmund had no beneficent hand to point out to him the shining treasures of real poetry with which our English literature abounds, so he had to rely on the titles in the catalogue of the Thanshope Free Library, and often received a stone instead of bread, in the shape of such jingling nonsense as he was greedily listening to just now.

Myles was a great reader of politics and

science. The romantic and poetic side of his nature had been left to itself; the soil, whether sterile or fruitful, had never received the least touch of cultivation—yet. He had some strong convictions on the subject of ethics, which will be best left undescribed, to display their results in his actions as circumstances put his theories to the test.

There was something striking and uncommon in the appearance of all three of this group of brothers and sister. Mary was comely—a tall, well-formed, well-grown young woman, with the pale but clear and healthy complexion, dark eyes and hair of her elder brother—a calm, sensible face, not destitute of a certain still, regular beauty, but lacking the impetuousness and intensity of Myles's expression. She sat knitting a long grey woollen stocking, and looked with a large steady gaze now at Myles, now at Edmund, whose face was equally sharp cut as his brother's, but worn and drawn with pain and ill-health.

Edmund was nineteen; Mary two and twenty; Myles six and twenty; another, born between them, had died an infant.

At this juncture the back door was heard to open. Some one entered, and in the pause made by Myles in his reading there was distinctly audible a heavy sigh—almost a groan. Glances were exchanged between Myles and Mary; both looked as if they braced themselves to meet some ordeal. Edmund's face darkened visibly.

'Is that you, mother?' called out Mary cheerfully.

'Ay, it's me!' replied a rather grating voice—a voice high, though not loud, and complaining in the midst of an ostentatious resignation.

'Go on, Myles!' said Edmund, in an undertone.

'Can't, my lad. You know mother can't abide it.'

'Why am I never to have a bit o' pleasure? It's precious little as I get,' grumbled the lad, as he turned away, and lay with his face concealed.

'See, lad! Tak' the book, and read for thysel',' said Myles, who indulged in a tolerably broad dialect when in the bosom of his family.

Edmund shrugged his shoulders irritably and made a gesture of aversion. Myles closed the book, rising from the side of the couch and going to the table, as a woman came in from the back kitchen—a small, sharp-featured woman, comely yet, with a bright cheek and a dark eye. She was the mother of all those tall children, though she was only five and forty, having been married, as too many of her class do marry, at eighteen. The great wonder was that she had remained a widow so long, for in addition to good looks, clever fingers, and a stirring disposition, she possessed property to the extent of thirty pounds per annum, left by a rich relation to her years ago.

An ignorant observer, looking at the family party just now, would have said what a good-looking, prosperous, well-to-do party they were. But Mrs. Heywood had scarcely spoken yet.

'Evenin', mother,' said her eldest son civilly, but, it must be owned, hardly cordially.

'Good-evenin',' she returned, in her high-pitched, dubious voice. 'What! you've managed to get th' tea ready, lass? But I know what that means. Just twice as much tea in the pot as we've any need for, or as I should a' put in mysel'. Waste, waste, on every side!'

As this was Mrs. Heywood's invariable remark when she came in from her occasional day's sewing at one of the large houses of the neighbourhood and found the tea prepared, it excited neither comment nor indignation, and the excellent woman, seating herself, cast a sharp, discontented look around, as if wishing that some one would give her

an opportunity of saying something disagreeable.

'Eh, bi' the mass! It is some and hot!
If some folks had to walk as far as me, may-
hap they'd understand what I feel at this
moment.'

Again no answer. Myles was buttering
a piece of bread. His eyebrows were contracted again. The serpent in that Eden
was the contentious woman. Myles never
answered her complaints, on principle, for
fear of saying something outrageous and un-
becoming, but it was often with a sore
struggle that he abstained : he did not want
to become a household bully, or he knew—
he had found it out by accident one day—
that a certain look and tone of his could
quell Mrs. Heywood's temper in one minute.
He was very much afraid of using it too
frequently, though often sorely provoked.
'Such people as Sebastian Mallory,' he reflected (whose mother was said to live for
him and his happiness), 'were not obliged to

stay in one room, listening to maddening complaints, like the continual dropping of a rainy day, with no alternative but solitude, silence, or the taproom.'

Edmund's shoulders were drawn up to his ears, and his back expressed distinctly that he felt himself jarred and grated in every fibre of his being.

'Now, then, Edmund,' said his mother, in her thin, penetrating voice; 'art comin' to the table, or mun thou have thy tea carried to thee, to drink on th' sofa, like a lady, eh?'

Answering to this appeal, he raised himself, his face darkened, his lips quivering with anger.

'That's right!' said he bitterly. 'Do insult me a little more! It's so nice to be ill, and so pleasant to spend your days by yourself upon a sofa in a kitchen. I'm likely to keep it up as long as ever I can. So would you if once you knew how agreeable it was.'

He had supported himself by means of a stick to the table ; and as he limped along to the chair which Mary had placed for him, one could see how much deformed he was, and how clumsily he moved. No look of pity warmed the woman's face as she saw him. He was not, like many a weakly or deformed child, the object of the mother's divinest love and tenderest care. He had been born three months after his father's sudden death. Mrs. Heywood had never been noted for enthusiastic devotion to any of her children, or to her husband, or, indeed, to any one but herself and her own interest. Myles could influence her ; but she seemed to have a positive aversion to Edmund, who used to say that his real mother was Mary.

When the meal was over, there was a little movement. Edmund looked wistfully towards Myles and the book ; but Myles did not offer to resume it. He had begun to think over that conversation in the office before pay-time, and was wondering whether it could be really true that Sebastian Mallory meant to return.

Sebastian Mallory was, and had been for years, his *bête noire*. He had seen him once, ten years ago, a handsome, fair-faced, 'yellow-haired laddie' of sixteen, who had come to look round his own works, with a somewhat listless gaze. Myles's vigorous soul had been filled with contempt for him at that moment, and he had never seen fit to alter that feeling. All he heard of Sebastian Mallory was exactly contrary to his ideas of what a *man*—unless the man were some irresponsible person, with neither business nor estate in the background—ought to be and do. He had a very strong sense of duty himself, and never, so far as he knew, left a duty unperformed. He struggled hard, according to his light, to do what was right; consequently he felt himself in a position to be somewhat censorious upon those who, he considered, obviously did not fulfil their duties—duties to their property, their dependents, their privileges, to him—Sebastian Mallory. Therefore he smiled somewhat grimly to himself as he imagined that lily-handed, yellow-haired, delicate-looking, young man coming to take his place at the head of affairs at such a crisis as was striding towards Lancashire—a storm which it would take the keenest heads, the strongest hands, the most practised eyes of the wariest business men who should succeed in weathering it. Probably Mr. Sebastian Mallory, if he did come, would cut a sorry spectacle, and would soon be glad to retire again to more congenial scenes abroad.

He did not feel it his duty to excite Mrs. Heywood's disagreeable remarks by reading aloud what he justly considered 'balderdash' to Edmund; he therefore suggested that they should go and take a turn on the Townfield.

Edmund, who for some reason was in a more unhappy temper than usual, shrugged his shoulders, and said he did not feel inclined to go out.

4—2

'No? Then I must go by myself, I suppose,' said Myles.

But he made no immediate effort to leave the house. He seated himself at the table with a book, and might possibly have remained in the house, but for his mother, who, having ascertained that his book was entitled 'The History of Rationalism,' announced that the bitterest grief of her declining years consisted in having to see a son of hers growing up an infidel, or worse. She hunted under the Family Bible, and produced a tract, which she offered him in lieu of the work he was reading. It bore the alluring title, 'Thou also, Worm!' And on his refusing this tit-bit of religious badinage, she put it aside with a bitter smile, and an audibly-expressed hope that it might not in the future go too hardly with those who had spurned the means of grace proffered by a mother's hand.

Myles endured these, and a succession of similar remarks, for some little time, while he

appeared to go on with his book without heed-
ing them ; but, as none knew better than she
who made them, the contracted eyebrows
and the impatient twisting of his moustache
covered considerable inward irritation. He
at last abruptly rose, and took his cap from
the nail on which it hung.

'Out again!' said Mrs. Heywood, in the
same maddening voice ; 'and if a mother
may ask, what pot-house are you going to
now ?'

'No thanks to you, mother, that I've not
taken to the pot-house long ago,' replied the
young man curtly, slapping his hat upon his
head, and leaving the room.

'If he doesn't break that door off its
hinges some fine day, in one of his tempers,
my name's not Sarah Ann Heywood,' remarked his mother. 'It's a grievous thing
to have an ungovernable temper. His Bible,
if he ever read it, would tell him that the
tongue is a little member, but a consuming
fire.'

'The Bible never said a truer word,' retorted Edmund witheringly; and Mrs. Heywood, returning to her knitting, with the
pleasant sense of having driven out the
strongest, sank into silence.

CHAPTER IV.

ADRIENNE.

'I love my lady; she is very fair;
    Her brow is wan, and bound by simple hair:
    Her spirit sits aloof, and high,
    But glances from her tender eye,
        In sweetness droopingly.'

MYLES left the house, and traversing some sideways, found himself presently in a steep, hilly street, which he descended, arriving at last, at a sort of square, through the middle of which ran the river Thanse, and on both sides of which were rows of shops. Then, walking on a hundred yards or so, he emerged in another still larger open space, opposite a large and beautiful building, which, in its delicate and multiform Gothic tracery, and noble dimensions, with the springing gilded spire leaping aloft at last, offered a startling contrast to its sordid surroundings—the shabby, low houses, narrow streets, and grimy factories which crowded round, as near as they dared. The river here made a bend, and passed the front of the town-hall. A kind of boulevard had been made, planted with trees, and immediately across the river, fronting the town-hall, was a house standing in a garden, divided by the river from the road. It was a fine old house of red brick, which had no doubt originally been 'in the country.' There was a look of stateliness and substance about it—the brick was relieved by handsome stone mullions, copings, and chimney-stacks.

The trees had been stunted by smoke, but they lived yet. Much ivy—strong and tenacious from advanced age, clung about it. The grounds were thoroughly well kept.

The parterres were blazing with the passion-
ate, glowing colours of late summer flowers ;
the windows were glazed with sheets of plate-
glass. Here and there a bow had been thrown
out. Behind were extensive stables and out-
houses. It was, though dingy, and miscellaneous in architecture, a fine, imposing old
mansion ; it instantly caught the stranger's
eye, and was known from infancy to every
inhabitant of Thanshope as well as the old
church on the hill behind the town-hall, or
as the great co-operative stores on another
hill at the other side of the town.

To-night Myles looked more earnestly than
usual at this old house. It was called ' The
Oakenrod,' and was the property of Sebastian
Mallory, tenanted during his absence by that
stately dame, his mother.

' There it is !' said Myles within himself.
' Cumbering the ground—kept like a palace
for a fellow who doesn't care two straws for
it !'

Again he shrugged his shoulders, and

turned somewhat abruptly to the left, making
for one of the side doors of the town-hall.
He went in, and ran up a great many flights
of stone steps, past corridors and branching
passages, till he could go no higher, for the
excellent reason that he was at the top of the
building.   Pushing open the glass door which
swung to behind him, Myles found himself in
the holy of holies—the library.   A door to
the right led into the reading-room, and
thither he directed his steps.   It was a large,
lofty, handsome room, with many tables and
chairs, and plenty of pens, ink, newspapers,
and periodicals scattered about.   When Myles
entered the room was almost empty.   One
or two men were reading newspapers, and at
one table in a window sat a girl, who had a
great book open before her, but whose eyes
were at the moment intently fixed upon the
old house, the Oakenrod, which lay directly
beneath.

Myles, searching about, found a number of
the *Westminster Review*, and took it to his

accustomed place, at the table next to that where the girl sat. He noticed no one to right or to left of him—not even she who was almost the only lady visitor who ever entered the reading-room.

She was already a familiar figure to his eyes. For some months past he had seen her nearly every evening, sitting at the same table, even at the same side of that table, with a book—generally some large and weighty volume, open before her—and a small, thick note-book, in which she wrote extracts or abstracts of what she read.

Myles knew quite well the tall, slim figure, the two dresses which she alternately wore— one a soft, flowing black one—another, soft and flowing too, of a blue so dark as to be nearly black. He knew that the lines of her dresses flowed gracefully, and were agreeable to the eye. He knew, too, the little black *fichu* which she usually wore— a sort of apology for a mantle, which she never discarded on the hottest days; the modestly-shaped white straw hat, with its carefully preserved black lace scarf, and bunch of daisies at one side, which hat she always ended in taking off after she had sat there ten minutes or so. She had a pale, clear, fair complexion, bright, warm chestnut hair, and a face which, not conventionally beautiful in outline, was full to overflowing of the subtler, more bewitching charm of a beautiful spirit. It—her face—had a youthful softness of outline—not full, but not thin, with a charming, rounded chin, melting into the full white throat; a mouth whose lines attracted irresistibly, so good, so spiritual were their curves; an insignificant but well-cut nose; a pair of large, luminous, expressive eyes, which in some favourable lights might appear grey, but which an impartial observer must inevitably have confessed, had a shade of green in them.

Myles and this young lady had sat at neighbouring tables in the public reading-room almost every evening throughout the

spring and summer months of that year.
Whenever Myles came into the room he had
found the young lady there ; he could not, of
course, tell whether she came when he was
not there.

Conversation in the reading - room was
against the rules ; but ' conversation ' is an
abstract noun of considerable indefiniteness,
and one to which different minds may attach
different meanings. A few words exchanged,
of greeting or courtesy, could scarcely have
come under the head of ' conversation,' or if
it did, the rules were infringed every day.
A little remark, as one passed the paper to
the other—fifty little things might have been
said (and were said by some frequenters of
the room) without in the least disturbing the
peace of the studious.

But between Myles and his neighbour
those words had never been spoken. They
had never exchanged a syllable—Myles because of a certain British-workman-like shy-
ness, and a general sense that she belonged,

despite the simplicity of her appearance, manner, and attire, to the class of 'fine ladies' whom he disliked and distrusted— the class which was typified for him in the person of Mrs. Mallory of the Oakenrod— and of whom he had the idea that they were silly, pretty, useless, expensive things, good for nothing but to spend a man's money, and make him miserable with their tricks and antics—and break his heart if he were fool enough to give it into their keeping—incapable of taking any part in the serious things of life.

That was his opinion of 'ladies.' For the women of his own class he had a hearty respect and admiration: they could earn wages; they could work; they did not meddle with things out of their sphere: they had a distinct use and purpose: he never uttered an ill-word to or of any one of them.

He had never spoken to his neighbour because he was shy, and did not know how to begin a conversation; but he would have

scorned to own it : he would have
said :

‘ Speak to her ?. Why should I speak to
her ? I've nothing that I want to say to
her.’

Which would have been untrue ; for there
was such intelligence, such sympathy in her
face that he many a time caught himself, on
reading any striking passage, wondering
what she would think of it if she had
read it.

She had never spoken to him, because—
why—because—well, what did it matter ?
possibly because she was a little more sensible than most girls, and felt no wish to
speak unless she had something to say.

They met without sign of recognition.
He would take his place—she hers : she
always had some book under her arm, for
which she had stopped to ask the librarian
on her way in, and they would often pass a
couple of hours thus almost side by side, without a word or a look. She read earnestly and

hard—not as if she read for pleasure, but for work—with a purpose. Privately, Myles was mightily puzzled to know what she could be reading, or rather, with what object she read what she did. Once he had been quite excited (silently) to see her poring over a musical score; reading it as if it were a book. One of the specialities of the Thanshope Free Library was its musical department, which was richly stocked both in scores and in treatises on music and musicians.

During the summer, the room was generally nearly empty. The people were otherwise employed, so that often not more than half a dozen readers were to be found in all the large, airy room—sometimes Myles and the studious, unknown 'reading girl' were all alone there.

Myles opened his Review, and his eye fell upon an article on the governing classes which instantly caught his attention. In the hope of finding some follies and weaknesses of the governing classes sharply castigated, he settled himself with pleased expectation to his book.

Half an hour passed. One by one the other occupants of the room walked away. The workman and the young lady were left alone together. She looked every now and then out of the window. Her note-taking did not seem to flow so smoothly as usual. Spread open on the table before her, she had a fine edition of the 'Fugues' of Domenico Scarlatti, which she studied a little now and then, but oftener looked out through the window. Now, from that window she had a tolerably wide prospect; and immediately beneath her eyes was the handsome old red-brick house, with its flower-beds, and its lawns, smooth, and green, and well-watered —a rural fastness in the midst of the dusty town.

There was silence that was almost solemn in the big room, which was growing dusk : it was so high and airy, and so isolated ; raised far above the town and its troubles; the din hushed; the rolling vehicles and the passing throng dwarfed; books on every side, and silence like a garment, over all.

As chimes broke that silence, and eight o'clock struck, the girl, with a sigh, turned resolutely away from the outside prospect, and applied herself again to her score.

Myles, half-roused by the chiming, half-pleased with a particularly hard hit at the governing classes, which especially took his fancy, raised his head at this moment, and his eyes, without any thought of his neighbour. It is a gesture which every one makes sometimes in reading. Smiling with satisfaction at what struck him as a masterly argument, Myles let his eyes fall upon her.

She too was looking up—not at him, but past him. Her eyes were turned towards the door, and quick as thought there passed a subtle, inexplicable flash of dislike tempered with alarm, across her face. She made a movement as if to rise—as if to escape ; then sat down again, with a flush, more of annoyance than confusion, mantling in her cheeks. Then, bending to her book, she seemed to make some effort to keep her eyes firmly fixed upon it.

This little bit of by-play roused Myles's attention. He turned his head towards the door, which was behind him, and he saw how it was opened, and a man came into the room. A gentleman ? he speculated, as he first saw the figure in the obscure background.

The visitor gradually approached, and Myles, staring unceremoniously at him, experienced a feeling of surprise, disgust, and sudden enlightenment as to the cause of the young lady's disturbance.

The new-comer was a young man with a somewhat high colour, dark hair and eyes, a full beardless face, and a coarse, animal mouth. He was well, even foppishly dressed, and bore the outward stamp of a person to whom money is not a subject of painful study or consideration. But, as Myles knew, he was not sterling coin. His manner, even of entering that room, was less than second-rate; confidence became a swagger; independence was metamorphosed into self-consciousness. The expression of his face was bold and vulgar. Perhaps no greater or more telling contrast could have been found, than that between the workman in his work-a-day dress, and the would-be dandy in his gloved, perfumed, over-dressed vulgarity.

This person came forward; his eyes fell upon Myles; he removed them. A workman—a person not demanding his attention, one of the 'fellahs' who came to the reading-room.

Nevertheless, he seated himself at Myles's table and drew a *Daily News* towards him, without speaking and without removing his hat.

Myles glanced at the young lady without letting her see that he did so; her eyes were fastened upon the page before her, but he had studied her expressions, and knew that she was not reading.

'Now, I should like to know,' speculated Myles inwardly, 'what you may want here, Mr. Frederick Spenceley?'

He had recognised the man—the son of a rich manufacturer of Thanshope, who had earned his fortune as a Radical, and was living in state now as a Conservative and a supporter of the aristocracy, Church, State, and landed gentry interest. His son, as Myles was well aware, had assuredly not visited the reading-room for purposes of mental instruction.

Myles apparently applied himself again to his book, but the argument had lost its charm for him. He had not known until now how lively was the interest he had taken in his graceful young neighbour. Placing his book so as to shield his face, but yet so that he could observe what was going on, he said to himself:

'I'm glad I didn't go away ten minutes ago.'

After bestowing a very short and scant meed of attention upon the *Daily News*, Mr. Spenceley cast his eyes around him. Myles watched him, and saw the leisurely impudence of the stare with which he favoured the young lady, and his ears began to tingle. He—my poor Myles—was of a fiery temperament, could not endure to see even a 'fine lady' insulted without cause, and was dangerously ready to take up the cudgels for the unprotected or ill-used.

'I beg your pardon,' said Mr. Frederick Spenceley, leaning towards the girl. 'Do you want that paper?'

He stretched his hand towards a newspaper which lay upon the table at which she sat, but he was looking at her with a stare, perhaps intended for one of gallant admiration, but which, from the unfortunate 'nature of the beast,' succeeded only in being impertinent.

Without looking at him, she raised her elbow from the paper on which it had rested, and continued, or seemed to continue, her reading.

'You don't want it?' he said, with what may have been meant for a winning smile.

'No,' came like a little icicle from her lips.

Myles with difficulty sat still; but, making an effort, continued quiet, though watching the game with a deeper interest than before.

The twilight had grown almost into darkness by this time. The attendant, perhaps not knowing that any one was in the room, had not yet lighted the gas.

Mr. Spenceley took the paper, but without even pretending to look at it, said, in a tone of under-bred badinage :

'Isn't it rather dark to be reading, Miss —a——'

She raised her eyes this time, and caught those of the speaker fixed full upon her. Her

own were instantly averted, with an expression of cold contempt and disgust, and she
made no reply.

'I assure you it's very bad for the eyes
to read by this half light — very trying.
Hadn't I better tell the fellah to light the
gas? I am sure you will spoil your eyes,
and that would be a pity,' with a winning
simper, which made Myles's fist clench with
an intense desire to do him some horrible
violence. 'Don't you really think I had
better?' he pursued, evidently bent upon
making her speak. At last he succeeded.

'Be good enough to mind your own business, without addressing me,' said she, in a
voice which, thought Myles, was sufficient to
have rebuffed the veriest cur that ever called
itself by the name of man.

With that she quietly, by slightly altering
the position of her chair, turned her back
upon Mr. Spenceley, while her profile, with
frowning brow and indignantly compressed
lips, was plainly visible to Myles.

Mr. Spenceley laughed, not so musically as a lady-killer should be able to laugh, and remarked :

'I feel it my business to prevent a young lady from spoiling her eyes, and——'

Steadying his voice with some difficulty into something like indifference, Myles turned to him, and said :

'Don't you know that talking is forbidden here ?'

The look which he received in answer made him smile, despite his inner indignation. Mr. Spenceley contemplated him with a stare, which was unfortunately not so regal as it might have been ; then, raising a single eyeglass, he stuck it into one eye, and surveyed the audacious speaker anew, as if his wonder at what had occurred could never be sufficiently satisfied.

'Will yah mind yah own business, and leave gentlemen to mind they-aws ?' he at last drawled out, with magnificent disdain.

'When I see the gentleman I shall be quite
ready to leave him to mind his own business,' was the placid retort. 'In the mean-
time, as the young lady wishes to read, and I
wish to read, and you disturb us with your
chatter, perhaps you will kindly hold your
tongue.'

Here Mr. Spenceley resolved upon a
master-stroke. Turning his broad-cloth clad
back, he tilted his chairback so as to see the
young lady better, and inquired :

'Do you know the fellah, Miss—a——?'

Before she could reply (supposing that she
had any intention of replying), Myles had
leaned a little forward and tapped Mr. Spenceley on the shoulder. With a great start,
quite disproportionate to the circumstances,
the latter brought his chair to its normal
position again. Myles saw the start, and
stifled a smile.

'Excuse me, my good sir, I don't remember ever to have seen you here before, so
perhaps you won't mind showing me your

ticket—I mean your member's ticket—otherwise——'

'Will yah hold yah tongue?' retorted the
other, in a tone of scornful exasperation.

'No,' replied Myles. 'If you've any right
to be here, show me your ticket, and hold
your tongue, according to rules; if you
haven't that right, walk out at once.'

'I can tell yah, yah don't seem to know
who yah speaking to,' observed Mr. Spenceley, apparently lost in astonishment. 'Are
yah one of the authorities here?'

'Oh, yes! I know you,' said Myles, who
saw that the young lady was now watching the dispute with undisguised interest.
'And I'm that much of an authority that I
can prevent you from disturbing and annoying people. Once for all, will you show me
your card of admission?'

'No, I won't.'

'Then you'll excuse my going to the
librarian, and telling him you are here without right—unless you prefer to save that

trouble to me, and ten shillings to yourself, by walking yourself off now, this moment,' said Myles, who began to find a delicious piquancy in the sensation of dealing thus summarily with a person of the consideration of Frederick Spenceley. It was an ignoble feeling, and we all have ignoble feelings sometimes, or what is the meaning of the constant injunctions to bear and forbear which we receive from different sources?

'Haw! Wha—at?'

'The fine for using this room without belonging to it is ten shillings. There's another fine for talking and disturbing people, too,' said Myles, who had never lost his look of perfect ease and calmness, and who did not for a moment remove his eyes from the other's face.

Mr. Spenceley did not appear to like the mention of fines. His face fell; his hand involuntarily sought his pocket.

'Tender in that direction, poor fellow!' thought Myles to himself.

'Confounded radical place, this!' observed Mr. Spenceley. 'Not fit for gentlemen to live in.'

'Not when they have only been gentlemen since the last general election,' said Myles politely. 'I quite agree with you.'

'Well, I shall go and see what the librarian says to all this,' said Mr. Spenceley, by way of covering his retreat; and then, after a prolonged stare at the girl in the window, he retired, not so jauntily as he had entered.

Myles picked up his book again. The girl watched her tormentor until the noiseless door had swung to behind him, and she had seen his shadow pass towards the stairs. Myles feigned to read, but he could not help seeing how she trembled as she sat there.

He did not speak to her. Something—he knew not what—held him back. But he suddenly felt a light touch upon his arm, and, looking up, saw the young lady standing beside him.

'Do you think he is really gone?' she asked, scarcely above her breath.

'Oh, yes! That sort of cur slinks off when you stoop for a stone, with his tail between his legs. It's only when he has his kennel well behind him that he turns upon you and snaps,' replied Myles, with homely if expressive metaphor.

She drew a long breath, raised her head again, and said, with a mixture of dignity and gentleness which appealed intensely to his strongest feelings of admiration :

'I cannot tell you how much I am obliged to you !'

'Don't mention it, miss,' said he; and it was odd that, while Mr. Spenceley's 'miss' made every right-minded person pant to knock him down and pound him well, Myles's 'miss' was not in the faintest degree offensive.

'You spoke as if you knew who he is; do you?' she added.

'Oh, yes! He's well enough known; he's

the only son of that Spenceley who has the big factories down at Lower Place—"Bargaining Jack " they call him.'

'Oh! I know who you mean. Poor man! How I pity him for having such a son !'

' Had you ever seen him before ?' asked Myles, confirmed in his impression that she was not a native of Thanshope, and finding conversation easier than he had expected.

' I have seen him several times lately. I seem always to be meeting him. Once I thought he had followed me, and then I thought how absurd to imagine such a thing; but he must have done it, all the same.'

Myles had had inexplicable sensations while she spoke. He had known her so long without a voice, that now, when he heard it, she seemed to become a stranger again ; and yet not a stranger. She had a sweet, low voice, clear and penetrating, and she spoke with an accent that had something not quite English in it.

It would have been difficult—to Myles, in
his ignorance, impossible—to say in what the
foreign element lay ; but it was assuredly
there. When she spoke, she looked at him
with fleeting glances which had nothing in-
sincere in them, and her face lighted up and
became lovely—and more than that, distinguished, spiritual ; the slender figure was
balanced with such a graceful poise ; the delicate hands were free from all nervous restless-
ness. Her chestnut hair was abundant, and
its dressing so simple and beautiful as alone
to make her remarkable. Myles realised
that she was most distinctly a ' lady,' but he
could not make himself feel her to be either
trivial or stupid. There had been nothing
trivial in her behaviour. Her treatment of
him flattered his discrimination when he remembered her late treatment of Mr. Spenceley. At that time of his life he had very
wrong ideas on the subject of gentlemen,
having mistaken notions as to their power
and character ; but the best part of his

nature was soothed and pleased when so perfect a piece of refinement as this young lady treated him entirely as a gentleman.

'And I thank you again, very much,' she added, smiling, and holding out her hand.

Myles forgot to be confused as he accepted the hand so frankly extended, and felt encouraged to do what he had thought would be right from the moment she had spoken to him.

'I am very glad to have been of service. May I ask how far you are going ?'

'To Blake Street, if you know it.'

'I know it well. It is too far for you to go alone, if you will excuse my saying so. It is quite possible that fellow may be hanging about yet. I'll go with you, if you will allow me ?'

'Oh! you are very kind,' said she, with visible relief. 'I cannot refuse, though I am sorry to take you away.'

'Not at all. I can't fasten to it again,' said Myles sincerely.

'Then, if you would be so good, I should be very grateful,' said she ; and she looked so relieved, and so pleased, that Myles felt himself rewarded an hundredfold for the act which had occurred to him as one of simple civility—nay, of almost obvious necessity.

They left the town-hall when she had returned her book to the librarian, and passed out into the street, turning to the right.

'This is the shortest way, miss,' said Myles, distracted as to what he should call her, feeling 'miss' disagreeable, he hardly knew why, but, despite the wealth of the English language, having no other alternative than a bald 'you.'

She relieved his mind as if she had understood his thoughts.

'My name is Adrienne Blisset,' said she. 'I should like to know yours, if you will tell it me ?'

'Myles Heywood.'

'I like it—it is so English, so Lancashire.'

'It's not like yours, then,' said he. 'It sounds foreign.'

'Adrienne? Yes; that is French for Adriana; but I pronounce it in the German way—Adrien-ne. Don't you see?'

'I never heard such a name—for an English young lady,' said Myles simply.

'I am not altogether an Englishwoman. I am half German. I was never in England till eighteen months ago.'

'Never in England!' echoed Myles incredulously. 'Then you speak English amazingly well.'

Adrienne laughed, and Myles asked:

'How do you like England now that you are in it?'

'I do not know England. I only know Thanshope, and I—cannot say—that I do like it much—if you will excuse me.'

'Oh, we don't expect every one to like our town,' said Myles magnanimously. 'It is a rough sort of a place, I fancy. And I should not think you would like it, either.

You are not like most of the ladies here.'

' No ?'

' There isn't another lady in the place who would come to the reading-room as you do.'

' Indeed. Why ?'

' They are too fine, I suppose,' said he contemptuously.

' Too fine ?'

' Ay. We have a lot of fine ladies here. There's Mrs. Spenceley, mother of that fellow who was annoying you this evening; but she's not so fine, certainly, poor thing ! But there's her daughter !' Myles shrugged his shoulders and turned his eyes to heaven.

' Is she very fine ?'

' Whenever I see her she is as fine as fine can be ; but perhaps she has some excuse for it, for she is very handsome, and she has a kind face too ; one would wonder how she could be that fellow's sister. Then there's Mrs. Shuttleworth, that has the grand yellow

carriage, but she is better than some of them;
and she looks ill, poor thing! so perhaps her
finery only gives her very little comfort.'

'It seems to me that you have an excuse
for them all,' said Miss Blisset.

'Perhaps I have—for all but one—the
proudest and the finest of the whole lot. I'd
rather have any of them than her—and that's
Mrs. Mallory of the Oakenrod.'

'Mrs. Mal——' began Adrienne quickly,
and then stopped abruptly. 'Do you know
her?' she added.

'I know this much of her, that I work in
their factory, and she comes looking round
now and then, behaving as if she thought that
I, and the factories, and the town, and the
world in general were made for her pleasure
and service. Oh, she's a proud, insolent
woman, Mrs. Mallory; all the Mallorys are
proud and insolent. It would do them good
to be humbled, and I hope they will be.'

'Oh! how can you be so bitter against
them?' said she, as if shocked.

'No, I'm not bitter; but I don't like to see people like that giving themselves airs, looking as if the world's prosperity depended upon their continuing to favour it by living in it, when any one knows that if they had their bread to earn they couldn't do it. I like justice.'

'Justice, and a little generosity with it,' said she gently, smiling in what appeared to Myles a very attractive manner.

'We are here in Blake Street,' said he; 'which way do we turn?'

'To the right, please. My uncle's house is at the very end of the street.'

'The end—it must be lonely,' observed Myles.

'Yes, it is, rather. He lives at Stonegate.'

'Stonegate!' echoed Myles. 'I've often wondered who lived there, and never knew. Why, it is part of the Mallorys' property,' he said suddenly.

'Yes; I believe it is,' she replied composedly. 'My uncle has lived there for ten years now.'

There was a little pause, and then Myles said :

'You will excuse me, but I don't really think it is fit for you to walk all that long way of an evening, especially now that it gets dark so soon, and after what has happened to-night.'

'I suppose I shall have to give it up. Luckily I am nearly at the end of my task. So I shall try to finish it.'

'Your reading?' he said inquiringly.

'Yes. References for my uncle's book. He is writing a book about Art and the Development of Civilisation : he is too infirm to go to the library himself, and I like going there. I have been reading up music for him all summer.'

'Oh, that's it!' said Myles, in a tone which betrayed ingenuously enough that he had thought often and deeply upon the subject.

'Yes, that is it. I must really try to go a few times more, because those books may not be removed from the library; and then I shall not need to go any more.'

'But you have not been here long, you said?' said Myles.

'No. Only eighteen months, since my father died abroad, and my uncle asked me to come and live here with him, else I should have had no home.'

She spoke with a quietness amounting to sadness, and Myles felt sure that there was sadness in her life, though she spoke so cheerfully.

'Were you sorry or glad to come to England?' he ventured to ask.

'Oh, sorry. Every association I had with it was unpleasant; whereas I had had many pleasures at different times abroad; and it is so cold, and dull, and *triste* here.'

'For any one that has no friends——' he began.

'Like me,' she said.

'It must be rather dull. Here is your place, I think.'

'Yes,' said Adrienne, pausing with her hand on the latch of the gate. 'I would ask you to come in, only it would disturb my uncle so much. But I shall see you again, and another evening I hope you will come in—will you?'

'You are very kind,' said Myles, secretly feeling immensely flattered at the invitation. 'If it wouldn't be intruding——'

'Not at all. I should like to know what you think about one or two things. I know you think, by the books I have seen you reading, and I have a burning curiosity to know what you think.'

Myles suggested that his subjects—work, wages, politics—might not be very interesting to a young lady.

'It depends so much upon the kind of young lady, I think,' said she, smiling. 'Well, good-night; I am obliged for your kindness.'

With a gracious inclination of her head she was gone—had passed swiftly up the walk, opened the door, and entered the house.

Myles stood for some time on the spot where she had left him, staring at the house. He looked at it well. 'Stonegate, Blake Street.' The whole of Blake Street was part of the Mallorys' property—Sebastian Mallory's property, to gain which he had toiled not, neither had he spun; but it had come to him, and was his to do as he would with.

Blake Street was a long street, composed, for about half its length, of smallish houses, in which lived quiet, steady, proper people. Several of the door-plates bore the indications of dressmakers; there were two dentists, a veterinary surgeon, and an undertaker. The rest were quiet, dull, dingy-looking private residences.

Beyond a certain point all this changed. Blake Street became a mere confusion of pasteboard terraces, half-finished houses,

single strips of houses, and general disorder
and chaos—a brick and plaster abomination
of desolation. And then came a lonely
stretch of street, quite without houses, with
an unfinished footpath on either side, skirt-
ing a waste of what really had been heath,
and was now little else. Some tufts of
heather might be found growing there in
their season, and the air that blew over it
was sharp and keen.

Across this common one might see the
lights of the town; dim outlines of factories
and churches, and masses of buildings—the
tortuous lines of light creeping up steep
streets and lanes, and the indistinct outlines
of the long range of the Blackrigg moors.
On the left side of the road stood one soli-
tary house, in a moderately-sized garden—
the Stonegate where Adrienne lived with her
uncle. It was an old house of dark grey
stone; square, solidly built, and of mode-
rately large proportions. It was contem-
porary with the Oakenrod, and had been

built by some far-back, dead and gone Mallory (they were lords of the manor of Thanshope) as a dower-house. In the garden the trees were shrivelled up, the flower-beds were adorned with nothing but a few evergreen bushes, and the grass was not kept as was the grass in the Oakenrod garden.

Behind the house was the lonely-looking waste of heath or common, which was out of Sebastian Mallory's jurisdiction; and in front a low wall with a wicket-gate in it, bounded the garden. From the wicket to the door was a flagged walk, raised a little above the grass border on either side of it. On each side the door two windows; on the second story five windows. The shutters of the lower windows were closed—the whole face of the house presented a blank, staring void, till at last Myles, looking intently upwards, saw a light appear in one of the upper windows and a shadow pass the blind. That must be Adrienne's room. Then he glanced at the surroundings of the house.

'A lonely place enough!' he decided within himself. 'I'm glad I came home with her. If that blackguard had been at the trouble to follow her! I hope he doesn't know where she lives: it hardly looks as if he did, or he wouldn't have chosen the public library to molest her in. I don't believe that if she called out, in this street, any one would hear her; and if they did, they're a poor lot— tailors, and women, and 'pothecaries: they wouldn't know a woman's screaming from a cat's miauling.'

'It is a nasty place!' he muttered again to himself, lingering unaccountably, reluctant to go. 'It looks as if there were a blight, or a curse, or something, upon it.'

At last he tore himself away, and took his homeward way.

CHAPTER V.

PHILOSOPHY AND FASCINATION.

'A tenderness shows through her face,
And, like the morning's glow,
Hints a full day below.'

MYLES walked home, not in the 'kind of dream' proper for a hero under the circumstances, but thinking very lucidly and very connectedly during his pretty long walk, from the end of Blake Street to his house on the Townfield, chiefly of what had happened that evening. He thought of Adrienne—of all those summer months of silence, and then of the sudden, quick acquaintance.

'She's certainly different from other .

people,' he said to himself; and in that matter he was right, if he meant that she was not like the ordinary Thanshope lady. But the ordinary Thanshope lady had not been brought up as Adrienne Blisset had been, and Myles did not know then, what patient struggles with sorrow and poverty and adverse circumstances had made her what she was. At one and twenty she had lived in many lands, and her mind had come in contact with many other minds, often minds of a far from common order. Very few English girls in her class have had that experience at that age—nor would those who wish a girl to be innocent and happy desire such experience for her, if it had to be paid for with such a heavy guerdon of sorrow and suffering as Adrienne had paid for hers.

Myles knew nothing of that, he only saw the difference. He felt a curiosity about her, blended with some admiration. He admired her grace, her spirit, her sweet voice, her quick intelligence; and he thought a great deal about her as he walked home, and wondered if he should see her again to-morrow—if she would be as gracious as she had been to-night ; he thought of Frederick Spenceley, and classed him in his mind with ' Mallory and that lot,' and was glad, quite revengefully glad, that he had been able to treat him as he had done, and that was all.

Perfectly unexpectant, unconscious, unaware of the web which circumstances, past, present, and to come, were weaving about his head, he paced the well-known streets—a son of toil, the descendant of generations of sons of toil, but with a whole world dormant in him, or rather nascent—a whole realm of suffering : love, hope, grandeur, baseness, which this night had first stirred into a premonitory natal activity.

Saturday morning came, and work, and the business of life ; Saturday afternoon, and holiday. Myles and Mary walked home together about two o'clock ; and his sister looked at him more than once, as his head and his eyes turned quickly from one side to the other, so often that at last she said :

' Why, Myles, dost expect to see some one thou knows ?'

' Me—no !' said he hastily, and with a forced laugh. He had been half unconsciously looking for Adrienne, but in vain.

In the evening he repaired to the reading-room as usual. He went straight to his seat in the window ; but she was not there, so he picked up the *Westminster*, which no one had disturbed since last night, and resumed the article on the governing classes.

But he could not, to use his own expression, ' fasten' to it, until he heard the soft opening and closing of the swing-door in the background, and the faint sound, almost imperceptible, of a girl's light footfall and undulating dress, came nearer and nearer. Then, when he looked up, she was there, looking just the same as usual—which was surprising, after all his dreamy thoughts about her.

She bowed to him, with the smile which lent such a charm to her fair face. For she was fair, Myles decided, as he saw that look of recognition : and he was right. She was one of those women who are not anything, neither ugly nor beautiful, until one knows them, and then they are lovely for ever.

With the 'Good-evening' and the smile they exchanged, he felt at rest, and could turn to his book again, and read, and understand. For not yet did he know that he had met his fate—good or evil as the case might be ; there was a sweet, momentary pause before there came that fever of unrest which love must be to such men as he.

Miss Blisset made her notes, and studied her music with diligence, until nine o'clock came chiming from the steeple above their heads, and there rang out after the chimes, the music of the tune, ' Life let us Cherish !'

Adrienne put her books together, and rose.

' Mr. Heywood, I told my uncle about

what happened last night, and he told me to ask you to come and see him this evening. Will you ?'

'I shall be very glad to do so,' said Myles, looking up, pleased and somewhat surprised. He had thought Miss Blisset's gratitude to him natural, under the circumstances, and had quite supposed that she would treat him with friendliness afterwards ; but he had smiled at the idea of the uncle of whom she spoke troubling himself about him. If he let the girl take that disagreeable walk to the town-hall every evening, he was not likely to care much whether she were annoyed or not, so that his work was done. That was the conclusion Myles had come to ; and it was a conclusion quite in harmony with his character.

They left the hall together : it was Saturday night, and the streets were thronged with a rough-spoken, roughly-mannered Lancashire crowd, pushing and talking, and, too many of them, reeling about, with the absence of ceremony peculiar to them. They soon left the thoroughfare, and found themselves first in the narrow cross-lane, and then in Blake Street.

'Only one more evening,' said Adrienne, 'and then my work will be done; and I shall not need to come any more.'

'I'm glad to hear it,' said Myles abruptly.

'You like reading,' said Adrienne. 'Have you read much?'

'I don't think I have,' he owned frankly.

'The Thanshope library is not a bad one in its way,' she remarked. 'Rather behind the time though, in the matter of science and philosophy.'

'Well, you see, it's like the gentlemen who have the managing of it, I suppose,' said Myles apologetically. 'They are a little behind the time, too.'

'Fortunately they have been allowed to exercise no control over my department, the music, since it was all bequeathed by a good

and enlightened man to the town; and all
those worthy committee people had to do,
was to accept it gratefully, and find a room
to put it in. And then, too, I don't think
they would know anything about the orthodox and heterodox in such matters.'

' Is there orthodox and heterodox in
music ?' asked Myles.

' I should think so ! The adherents of the
different musical creeds are given to a " bear
and forbearance " equal to that of adherents
of different religious creeds.'

Myles laughed a little at this, and
said :

' Then I'm sure ignorance is bliss in that
case. We're somewhat overrun with parsons
in these parts. The women make so much
of them that they seem quite to lose their
understanding—what they have of it. But
the vicar—Canon Ponsonby—he is quite
different ; and he keeps a pretty tight
hand over his parsons. I've heard that
he shows them their place sometimes as if

they were schoolboys. He ought to have been a prime minister, ought Canon Ponsonby.'

'Yes, I know him,' said Adrienne. 'He and my uncle are great friends. He is a grand old gentleman.'

Here they turned in at the wicket of Stonegate; Adrienne opened the door, and Myles for the first time—not for the last by any means—stood within that sad-looking, lonesome old house.

It was a square, matted hall in which they stood; dimly lighted by a Japanese lantern, also square, hanging from the roof. On a great oaken table in the centre, stood a large, beautiful vase of grey-green Vallouris ware. Over the carved mantelpiece hung an oilpainting—a fine copy of that beautiful likeness of Goethe—the one with the dark rings of curling hair, and the magnificent face; that likeness which always reminds one of the *herrlichen Jüngling* described by Bettina as the hero of a certain skating scene, when

he stole his mother's cloak—*der Kälte wegen.*
Opposite to this picture stood, on a pedestal,
a bust of Orfila. These were the only orna-
ments in the place : every other available
corner was filled with book-shelves loaded
with books. A dome-light gave light by day
to this hall.

'This way,' said Adrienne, opening a door
to the left, and Myles followed her into the
room. This room too was lighted with
lamps and candles. There was a table in
the centre—a writing-table in one of the
windows, piled with books, and papers, and
MSS. In an easy-chair, beside this writing-
table, reading, was a man—presumably the
'uncle' of whom Adrienne had so often
spoken.

'Uncle,' said she, going up to him, and
touching his arm, 'here is Mr. Heywood,
of whom I spoke to you.'

He looked up, and Myles beheld a strange,
long, pale face, with hollow eyes, and a large
and, as it seemed to him, an expressionless

mouth. It was a deathlike face ; its expression neutral to impassiveness.

'Mr. Heywood—oh, I am glad to see you.
Take a seat.'

Somewhat chilled by this unenthusiastic
greeting, Myles complied without a word,
feeling remarkably small and insignificant,
while Adrienne produced her papers, sat
down at the desk, and began to arrange
them. Mr. Blisset turned towards her, but
did not move his chair. He merely observed
to Myles :

'You will excuse us a moment, Mr. Heywood,' and then gave his attention to the
remarks which his niece, in a low tone, made
to him. It was with a kind of shock that
Myles soon perceived the man's lower limbs
must be paralysed. That was what Adrienne
meant when she spoke of his being unable
to come to the library. That was why he
was so shy and reserved that he must be
prepared for the visit of a stranger. Myles
understood it all now, and, from his ex-

perience of Edmund, knew what it meant, only that this was far worse, far more of a living death than that in which Edmund lived.

The writing and reporting over, Adrienne left the room. Myles and the strange-looking, corpse-like man were left alone; and now Mr. Blisset turned to him and said, still in the same cold, measured voice :

'You rendered a very kind service to my niece last night, and I am much obliged to you.'

'Pray don't mention it. No one could have sat still and seen a young lady annoyed by a fellow like Frederick Spenceley.'

'Spenceley — surely I have heard the name !'

'Very likely. His father is the richest man in Thanshope.'

'Oh—ah ! Naturally I have heard of him then. So that was the name of the individual who insulted her ?'

'That is his name,' said Myles concisely,

' and it's another name for a cad and a black-guard.'

' Oh, is it ? You know something about him ?'

' There are few people in Thanshope who don't. He is a born ruffian—Spenceley. Some day the ruffianism will come out through the veneering, and once out, it will never be polished over again.'

Mr. Blisset assented half-inquiringly, surveying Myles all the time from his impassive eyes, and then he said :

' I am sorry my niece should have to go to the reading-room. She tells me that one evening more will finish what she has to do, otherwise I should not permit it. But I should think you have frightened the fellow away for a time ?'

' Oh, yes ! He won't trouble her again,' said Myles, with contemptuous indifference, forgetting that beaten-off insects, with or without stings, have a habit of returning with blundering persistency to the attack.

'But couldn't she go in the daytime?' he asked suddenly.

Mr. Blisset shrugged his shoulders.

'There is so much work to be done in the daytime,' said he—'correspondence, and reading, and manuscript to copy. But I spare her as much as I can. I never ask or wish her to work after she returns in the evening. The rest of her time is her own.'

'I should hope so!—from nine o'clock!' thought Myles, a little surprised. 'She must be ready to go to bed at ten, after such a day as that. I wonder at what time it begins. Why, I am better off than that.'

'The rest of her time is her own,' repeated Mr. Blisset, as if he clung to that concession with fondness and pride, feeling that it made up for all other privations which her day's work might entail—which indeed was the case. His infirmity—his long confinement to one house and one spot—the absorbed concentration of his faculties upon one work

—a work which he was determined should burst upon the world, and make him illustrious—all this, and above all, Adrienne's own devotion to him and his pursuits, since she had come to live with him, had fostered his natural egotism ; till now he verily believed that his yoke was easy and his burden light to the young creature who bore it, and that that hour 'after she came in' was an elastic period, in which any amount of private work and reading could be done, and pleasure enjoyed.

Yet he was not a hard-hearted man, and if Adrienne had been by any cause removed from him, it would have been her gentle presence, and the charm of her company that he would have lamented—not the loss of her services in reading, writing, and research.

His intense and almost forbidding coldness of manner was soon understood by Myles, who discovered before long that it arose chiefly from physical weakness and languor—

not from any want of interest in the questions of the day, or in the men and things about him.

'You are writing a great book, sir?' inquired Myles, by way of something to say.

'A book,' corrected Mr. Blisset—a slight but ineffable smile playing upon the marble of his face. 'Let no men and no generation call any of their own achievements—whether in literature or legislation—great. That is for posterity to decide.'

('Humph!' thought Myles. 'That implies that posterity will take some notice of it, in which case—' but the reflections opened up were too large to be fully followed out then.)

'One branch of knowledge, and one alone, can produce works which at the very time of their appearance may be safely pronounced great — and that is science, of course,' resumed Mr. Blisset, half-closing his eyes.

'Then yours is not a scientific work,' said Myles politely.

'It is chiefly historical and speculative, but based, I trust, on the truest and most profoundly scientific principles.   It is an inquiry into the question whether highly advanced civilization and an art-spirit living, original, and capable of producing new and great works, can exist together—whether they are ever likely to go hand in hand.'

'And what do you conclude?' asked Myles.

'I began in hope,' said Mr. Blisset.   'But the hope has died away.   Music still remains —a wide, only partially-trodden field, but for the rest——' he shook his head.   'Of course it is a gigantic undertaking,' he went on, 'and I have been engaged upon it for twenty years.   But I think, when my work is complete, that I shall have pretty well exhausted the subject.'

'And your readers too, perhaps,' thought Myles, unwillingly forced to wonder whether there were much use in Mr. Blisset's gigantic undertaking.

At this juncture Adrienne came into the room again; and Myles, beholding her for the first time in indoor dress, was sensible of a warmer, deeper feeling of admiration than he had hitherto experienced. There was a nameless foreign charm about her, which worked like a spell upon him. She held some trifling work in her hand, and coming quietly in, seated herself, and lent her attention to her uncle as he went on discoursing in a monotone which by degrees fascinated Myles, so that he listened intently, and *nolens volens.*

It was only afterwards, in thinking it all over, that he remembered what a sad, dreary life it must be for the young girl, alone with this stupendous egotist, listening while he discoursed of—himself; helping him in his great work; writing letters relating to his vast undertaking; studying hard in order to supply him with facts. That was all true;

but at the moment Myles did not think of it, for Mr. Blisset spoke upon subjects that the young man had thought about himself—subjects that made his heart burn—of governments and peoples, and the lessons which history may teach us.

And when Myles heard the treasures of learning and research which Mr. Blisset had undoubtedly accumulated, brought to bear upon his own view of the question, and found that the speaker too was one of those whose watchword is—

'The people, Lord! the people!
Not crowns and thrones, but *men !*'

his admiration speedily grew to enthusiasm, and he sat listening, his handsome face all flushed with eagerness, and was disposed, before the evening was over, to rank Mr. Blisset as a demigod.

Mr. Blisset was pleased, like other philosophers, with the admiration he excited, and surveyed the young man with a favouring eye.

'You must come and see me again,' said he. 'It is always a pleasure to me to know one who has thought and felt upon these subjects. But I have talked till I feel almost exhausted. Adrienne, my love, suppose you give us some music.'

'Yes, uncle,' said she; 'I like you to talk in that way,' she added, touching his forehead with her lips. 'Then you do yourself justice.'

There was a piano in the room, and Adrienne's playing for her uncle when the day's work was quite over—a sort of requiem upon the toil they had passed through—was as regular a thing as the falling of night upon the earth. There, in the world of harmony, was her kingdom—there she ruled; from thence she could sway the hearts of men.

The harmonies she made for them that evening were calm and grave — a pathetic *Tema* of Haydn's; a solemn *Ciaconna* of Bach's; a slow movement, the 'singing together of the morning stars,' of Beethoven's.

Mr. Blisset shaded his long pale face with

his long pale hand, and sat, with closed eyes, listening. Myles was listening too, but ear, with him, was subservient to eye, and to thought. His gaze never left Adrienne, and the longer he looked, the deeper became the charm. There had slumbered in his mind, throughout these years of toil and striving, a latent, dormant ideal of loveliness, purity, and fitness for worship, and it was as though, when Adrienne's fingers touched the keys, that the door of heaven was opened, and a ray, falling upon her fair head, proclaimed her his soul's dearest wish.

With a sigh, promptly repressed, he rose from his dream as she finished, and took his departure, after Mr. Blisset had made him promise to come again.

It was Saturday night, and Myles found the din of the town not yet hushed. He saw sights which were familiar enough to his eyes, heard sounds to which his ears were accustomed—drunken men reeling out of the public-houses which must be closed, brawling songs shouted hoarsely up and down—all the ugliness of rude, coarse natures taking their pleasure. He had never in his life found pleasure himself in such things ; but equally, he had grown accustomed to the fact that others—men with whom he was on good terms — did take pleasure in them. He thought of the scene he had just left, and there shot a sudden sense of chill doubt and discomfiture through his frame of musing, high-strung happiness, a desperate feeling that those whom he saw about him in the streets now, were his class, his companions ; that, ever since he had begun to hope and think, he had hoped for their advancement, their good, and he must not be untrue to them.

'Pah !' said he to himself, ' as if she could ask a man to be false to what he ought to be true to. She's like truth itself.'

CHAPTER VI.

FINE LADIES AND FOLLY.

MONDAY morning, with the business of this work-a-day world in full swing, or rather in preparation for the week's swing of labour. In the freshness and rawness of a six o'clock morning air, Myles walked with his sister to his work. He and Mary were accustomed to do all their private conversation during these walks. They sometimes discussed their mother and her doings, and the discussion took away from the bitterness which silence would have left to rankle there.

To-day, Myles was exceedingly silent, but Mary, who knew him and loved him better than any other soul, felt that the silence was no sign of dejection.

The brother and sister separated, on arriving at the factory. Mary went to the weaving shed, and Myles to the warehouse. After breakfast the same arrangement took place; but the day was not destined to be one of pleasant memories for Myles.

In the course of the forenoon he was in the outer office, with Wilson the overlooker, when the latter, glancing through the window, remarked :

'There's Mrs. Mallory coming. I see her carriage.'

Myles made no answer, for the information did not seem to him of any particular importance; but Wilson went on, in a voice which had grown, by anticipation, smooth and respectful.

'I expect she wants to see Mr. Sutcliffe,

and he's out. So she'll have to put up with me.'

With that he stepped up to a square of looking-glass, which he retained despite all Myles's gibes and jeers, over the mantelpiece, and smoothed his hair.

'And, Myles, lad, as Mrs. Mallory's coming, and may have business to speak about, perhaps you'd better——'

'Go?' said Myles tranquilly, though the suggestion was highly irritating to him. 'That I'm not going to do, old chap. I've got these figures to write down ; and here I stay and write them, if fifty Mrs. Mallorys were coming.'

Wilson made no answer. Myles's position was too near his own for him to be able to order him out of the office ; but, not quite satisfied, he waited, snatching up bundles of papers and sample cops, shoving an empty skip aside, and endeavouring to make the rough office look a little tidier.

'What a pity,' remarked Myles sarcas-

tically, 'that you haven't got a few ever-
greens and some paper roses. I'd invest in
a few if I were you, and keep them in the
cupboard, ready for such an occasion as
this.'

With which he seated himself at the desk
in the window, which commanded a view of
the street, and began to write.

Wilson walked up and down, watching the
carriage as it drew nearer, and Myles felt
contemptuous and superior.

'She's got Miss Spenceley in the carriage
with her,' observed Wilson, reconnoitring
over Myles's head. 'They go a deal together, those two.'

Myles looked up sharply as he heard this.
The carriage had stopped; Wilson had rushed
to open the door. Myles saw the open
carriage standing at the gates, and how one
lady sat waiting while the other got out.
The face of the waiting lady was turned towards the office.

'Miss Spenceley'—the sister of the man

who had displayed his contemptible character
to Adrienne Blisset the other night. It was
not likely that Myles should glance at her
with very amiable or respectful feelings. He
saw a graceful figure leaning nonchalantly
back in the carriage ; he had a general impression of a brilliantly beautiful brunette
face, large dark eyes, an extremely elegant
costume, a hat, or bonnet, with a waving
plume, a parasol covered with lace—and that
was all. But he had long sight; he saw
none of her brother's expression on the girl's
countenance, which was frank and open, as
well as beautiful.

'I'd bet something they don't get on well
together,' he thought ; and then he heard a
silk dress rustle over the threshold, and a
woman's voice answering indifferently Wilson's profuse salutations. Myles could not
help looking up, though he tried not to do
so. He had often seen Mrs. Mallory before;
but she had never seen him. Now she was
looking full at him.

She was a handsome woman, of some forty-six years of age, but looking younger when one did not notice certain lines about her eyes and mouth—lines of meanness as well as of pride. She was very richly dressed in black; there was silk, and lace, and perfume about her. She was tall, fair, pale, and inclined towards *embonpoint.* She looked Myles over from head to foot; then, turning to Wilson, said :

'Is Mr. Sutcliffe in ?'

'I'm very sorry, 'm; he isn't. He has had to go to Bolton, and won't be back till afternoon.'

'Oh !' said she, pausing as if in thought; and then added, 'Give me the papers Mr. Sutcliffe was speaking about the other day; they are sure to have been left ready. I will take them home with me, and look them over.'

Myles had turned again to his work, and was bending over a page of figures, wroth with himself that, instead of being able undisturbedly to add up the figures he had put down, he could not help listening to Mrs. Mallory's voice.

'Yes, 'm; I'll find the papers. They'll be in Mr. Sutcliffe's room. But won't you sit down 'm, while I look for them?'

'No; make haste, please,' was all she said, a little impatiently; for Mr. Wilson's manner was, to put it mildly, fussy; and Myles, feeling the influence of that tone, despite all his efforts, began to count half aloud:

'Three and five, nine—eight, I mean; and seven fifteen, and——'

'Here they are, 'm. Allow me to make them into a parcel, 'm; it will be more convenient.'

'No; you can take them to the carriage, and I will look them over when I have time.'

'Myles, lad, suppose you were to take the papers to the carriage,' said Wilson, wishing to appear superior.

Myles looked up, surprised ; he could read the simple, fussy character of the faithful old cashier to its very depths, and knew his motives exactly. He had no wish to disoblige him, and, with an amused half-smile, took the papers and walked to Mrs. Mallory's carriage.

The young lady, Miss Spenceley, was looking somewhat impatiently towards the office.

' Oh !' said she, when she saw Myles, ' is Mrs. Mallory in there ? Has she nearly finished her business, do you think ?'

Myles had seen the girl many a time before ; she was the beauty and the heiress, *par excellence*, of Thanshope ; the only daughter, as her brother was the only son, of her parents. The young man, looking at her more attentively than ever before, could find no trace of likeness, or his scorn of her relative might have displayed itself in his voice.

' I really don't know,' said he, in answer

to her question. 'She is talking to the cashier.'

'Oh, thanks!' said she, turning abruptly away, and looking impatiently up the street.

Myles returned to the office, and as he re-entered it Mrs. Mallory was saying to Wilson :

'Because I expect my son—your master—will be at home again shortly, and of course he will wish to inquire into everything that is going on.'

There was something in the tone in which this was said which rasped upon Myles's feelings—a calm superiority which he felt to be extremely needless.

'Then we may expect Mr. Mallory to come and take possession sometime soon?' Wilson hailed the news as if it were a personal favour.

'I expect so. I do not know the exact time ; but of course everything will be ready for him ?'

'Will *he* be ready for everything ?'

thought Myles, with strong contempt; his old spite — it deserves no nobler name— against the absent, unknown Sebastian Mallory rose angrily to the surface again. 'Our *master*, indeed!' he reflected angrily. 'I wonder if he's ever prvoed himself his own master yet?'

Wilson, by an unlucky combination of circumstances, was at this moment inspired to turn pointedly to Myles and remark :

'Now, Myles, do you hear what Madam Mallory says? I told you the master was coming, and you wouldn't believe me.'

'It remains to be seen whether "master" is the right word to use,' said Myles, with deliberation. 'In this case I have my doubts about it.'

He bent to his book once more, but not before he had seen the stony stare in the light blue eyes of Mrs. Mallory, and the gaze of haughty astonishment upon her pale, high-featured face—a stare which seemed to say, 'I have seen human nature in many obtrusive and ill-bred aspects, but never in one which so much required putting into its proper place as this.'

Myles smiled rather grimly to himself; he hated to exchange such civilities with any one, most of all with a woman, but his spirit could ill brook the unquestionably haughty and supercilious manner of Mrs. Mallory, and the profuse mouthing of the word 'master' by Wilson's complaisant lips. Myles had, up to now, utterly refused to call any man master, and he was not going to begin it in the case of a man whom he had never seen; and to whom local report gave anything but a decided or master-like character.

'There's no call for you to be so rude,' said the cashier, shocked and reproachful.

Myles turned to him.

'Will you understand,' said he, with lips that had grown tight, ' that a man can't both do arithmetic and talk ?'

'Who *is* the young man ?' inquired Mrs. Mallory of the discomfited Wilson.

'You must excuse him, 'm. He's one of the foremen : he knows no better.'

Myles made no sort of comment upon this apology, content that they should say what they liked about him, so long as they did not require him to acknowledge an unknown 'master.'

Mrs. Mallory, after another and a prolonged stare of the said haughty astonishment, which stare wasted itself upon the back of the delinquent, swept away, leaving Myles with his lips twisted into a fine sneer—an expression to which they were wont too readily to bend.

※　　　※　　　※　　　※　　　※

Myles's temper had assuredly not been improved by the occurrences of the morning. It was destined to be yet more severely tried before his return to work in the afternoon.

On leaving the factory he parted from Mary, as he had an errand in the town, and told her he would be home in half an hour

for dinner.   He did his errand, and took his
way home.   And as he arrived at his own
gate there came out from it a man whom
Myles recognised as a person to whom he
bore no friendly feelings.   He was named
James Hoyle, and was by trade a small
shopkeeper, in the stationery and evangeli-
cal-religious-book line : occasionally he acted
as a preacher of a denunciatory and inflam-
matory description ;. always he was a mis-
sionary—so, at least, he said.

To him and to his style of preaching and
piety Myles had a most thorough dislike ; he
believed him to be a hypocrite, and in this
case his dislike was well grounded enough,
and founded on facts.

' Good-morning, Myles.   The Lord bless
you !' observed Mr. Hoyle, holding out a
dingy, fat hand.   No lowest scum of the
Levites, of whatever section, whatever persuasion, could have looked, thought Myles,
sleeker, or more as if his sleekness were an
ill-gotten gain.

Out of tune as Myles was with all the world, this apparition and his tone of familiarity, was not of a kind likely to restore harmony to the jarring notes of his life's music. Drawing up his proud figure to its utmost height, and looking with his contemptuous eyes down upon the pudgy individual who addressed him, he said :

'Good-morning. I'll thank you not to make so free with my name. Who gave you leave to call me " Myles " ?'

He ignored the outstretched hand, having an objection to touching what he considered to be both literally and metaphorically dirty fingers.

Hoyle looked up at him, and his eyes twinkled.

' I've been taking spiritual counsel with your mother, my dear young friend. A sweet, precious soul ! It is a privilege to converse with her ; she teaches one so much.'

' Does she ? It's a pity but she could

teach you to be sober and honest,' said Myles, with distinct enunciation and scornful mien, holding himself somewhat aloof from Mr. Hoyle. 'Anyhow,' he continued, 'until you've managed it—the soberness and honesty, I mean (you needn't look as if you didn't know. I saw where you came out of at eleven o'clock on Saturday night)—till then you'll please give this house a clear berth, and my mother may take her spiritual counsel—if she wants it—with a different sort of person from you.'

He was about to turn in at the gate, but, with his hand on the latch, was arrested by an expression on the face of the other.

'The day will come, young man, when you will wish you had treated me—me, of all people—with more respect,' said he with a smile, for he had a flexible face, which appeared to lend itself even more easily to smiles than to other expressions. Yet the smile was an evil one.

He turned and walked away, and Myles, in some annoyance, went into the house. Usually Mrs. Heywood had the field to herself in the exercise of her tongue. Edmund occasionally indulged in a burst of temper, but always to his own disadvantage. Mary never answered at all. Myles alone, as has been before said, could, with a certain look and tone, show himself master of the fretful, repining embodiment of scolding and selfishness whom they had the misfortune to call mother. To-day he was in no mood to 'stand nonsense,' and as he went into the kitchen he said, hanging up his cap, and taking Edmund's hand, as he seated himself beside him :

'What does yon James Hoyle want always hanging about here ? The chap is never out of the place, and I can't abide him. If he doesn't give us a little more of his room and less of his company I must speak to him. Mary, lass, I hope thou'rt not got agate of meeting-going.'

He spoke with perfect good-nature and good-temper, not suspecting anything but that all the rest of the company were equally averse with himself to Mr. Hoyle's visits, and he smiled a little as he looked at Mary.

'Me!' said his sister, laughing. 'Nay, I'm not come to that. As long as I live I'st go to th' parish church every Sunday, and sit in th' old place——'

'Alongside o' Harry Ashworth,' put in Edmund gravely, at which Mary's cheeks flushed, and she went on somewhat more rapidly :

'For I make nowt at o' out o' the meetin'-house.'

'Perhaps you'll end by leaving th' owd place for an older, and going clean over to Rome,' said Mrs. Heywood, who had been bending over the fire, looking at a pan of potatoes, and who now raised rather a flushed face from that occupation; 'choose how, there'st nowt be said here against James

Hoyle, the godly man! and it's more than likely that you'll see more of him than you have done yet.'

'How do you mean?' asked her eldest son, turning towards her; 'you mean that Jimmy Hoyle would come here a second time after I'd forbidden him the house?'

He laughed, as if he thought it rather a good joke.

'You'd turn him out of the house? That's like you!' said Mrs. Heywood, emptying the potatoes into a tureen.

'I really don't know what you're talking about,' said Myles, in some surprise at her whole demeanour.

'Well, you'll get to know, then,' she retorted, without meeting his eye. 'A good man is like the salt of the earth. He can make even a sinful house holy, and bring a blessing on it. James Hoyle and me is going to be married. We'st be wed this day three week, and then I'd like to know how you'll forbid him the house.'

There was a momentary silence, during which Myles, who had risen, stared at his mother in an incredulous manner. Mary, after a moment, turned pale, and sat down upon a chair in the background. Edmund's lips were curled into a sneer.

'Mother!' said Myles, confronting her, and somehow forcing her eyes to meet his. 'Is this a joke that you're playing upon us? Because, if so, it's a very poor one.'

'Joke!' she retorted, her voice rising to shrillness. 'What should it be a joke for, I'd like to know? Have I such comfort in my children that I shouldn't be glad of the help of a godly man—oh, and he is a godly man—like that?'

'That's a poor answer, mother,' said Myles, who had thrust his hand into his breast, as if to repress some anger or emotion. 'Your children have never done anything to cause you uneasiness.'

'Do go on blowing your own trumpet!' Mrs. Heywood exhorted him.

'Nay, I've no more to say about it. But I want a better answer than that your children's conduct drove you to marry that great, idle, greasy, sanctimonious, all-praying, no-doing brute—he isn't a man. I can understand him wanting to marry you—you've thirty pounds a year of your own; but that you should look at him !' He made an expressive gesture of contempt.

'So it's my money he's marrying me for,' said Mrs. Heywood; and no girl of eighteen could have spoken with more anger at the suggestion. 'That's it, is it? Ay, ay! "Honour thy father and thy mother,"—do !'

'Are you giving us an example of honouring our father?' he inquired, growing quieter in tone as his anger and disgust grew more intense, and her determination (he saw) more fixed. 'Or is your present plan likely to lead us to honour you? No, mother; I can't see what a woman like you wants with marrying again; though, if it had been a decent man, let him be never so rough, I'd have put up with him, but that—-why I saw him on Saturday night coming out of the lowest public-house in Thanshope—half-drunk—as plain as I see you. But here's the long and short of it. That man certainly never enters this house again. I'll let him know that. And if you do marry him, he'll please to find a home for you; for neither he nor you will share ours. Mark my words—if you go to him you leave us for ever.'

'Mother, thou'll ne'er be so wicked,' said Mary, from her corner, in tears.

'Hold thy tongue, thou hussy! calling thy mother wicked,' said Mrs. Heywood sharply.

'Ill not have Molly called by that name,' said Myles composedly. 'Remember, it's I that am master here, when all's said and done. I'll have no such nonsense carried on. So let us hear—do you intend to be a wise woman or a fool?'

The words were not at all rudely spoken,

but they were unfortunately chosen. They incensed Mrs. Heywood, and she replied sharply :

'I intend to marry James Hoyle.'

' Then,' said he slowly, as if giving her an opportunity to recant, ' it's settled that I intend to have no more to do with you.'

' Oh, Myles, don't be so hard on her !' implored Mary, coming forward and laying her hand upon his arm.

' My good lass,' said he, ' dry thy eyes, and be glad thou'rt not called upon to be hard, as thou calls it.'

Mary did not expostulate. Under the gentleness of the words she read a decision which she did not attempt to combat.

' Mary's our good angel,' remarked Edmund from the couch; and his eyes, too, fell upon her with affection.

' A nice angel you'll find her when I'm gone,' grumbled Mrs. Heywood.

' Once more,' broke in Myles's voice, ' I tell you, mother, I have spoken to you for the

last time, unless I hear that this abominable
thing is given up—for the last time.'

'Myles!' implored his sister. But she
might as well have tried to move one of the
great boulders on Blackrigg, as make him
soften or yield one jot.

'Come, lass!' he observed to her. 'Those
that must work must eat. The time's gone
by in this precious palaver, and we've only
twenty minutes left.'

He sat down and helped himself, and tried
to look as if nothing had happened; soon,
however, he laid down his knife and fork, and
told Mary, who had not even pretended to
eat, that it was time to go.

She put her shawl over her head, and saying good-afternoon to Edmund, they went
out.

CHAPTER VII.

SANS FAÇON.

SIX o'clock was the time at which the work-people 'knocked off.' Myles and Mary had not spoken as they went to their work, and of course not during the afternoon ; and it was only as they were coming home again that they first named the subject which at the moment lay nearest their hearts. Mary was all for mildness and temperate measures.

'I think, Myles, that if we was to be kind to her, and talk to her, hoo'd likely give it up,' said the girl, in her soft, broad Lancashire dialect.

'Not she, Molly. She's no intention of giving it up.'

'I never could abide yon Hoyle,' went on Mary. 'A false, sneakin' fellow, he always seemed to me. I reckon he's after mother's bit o' brass; but how hoo can gi' so mich as a thought to him—nay, it fair passes me!'

'Ay! you may well blush! I don't wonder!' said Myles grimly. 'It looks as if some people's minds were fair crooked, or set up on edge, or upside down, or some-thing.'

They went into the house, and found Edmund alone.

'She's not coming back,' said he, by way of salutation. 'She's gone to some of his relations. She says she's lived through a deal o' trouble, and has found out at last what it was to be turned out of doors by her own children.'

Neither Mary nor Myles made any answer to this announcement. Mary got tea ready, and they sat down. It was a silent, painful meal. Myles rose from it with a sense of relief, and, taking Edmund's book to change, said he was going down to the reading-room.

'Would thou mind calling at th' saddler's in Bold Street for yon strap o' mine?' said Mary.

'Which strap, Molly?'

'It's a girder as I took to have a new un made like it. He'll give you both th' old and th' new un. I could like to have it to take wi' me to-morn. I've been using Sally Rogers'; but hoo's comin' back again to-morn, and hoo'll want it hoo'rsel'.'

'Ay, I'll get it,' said Myles, putting on his cap and going out.

He made a little detour from his usual route, in order to go to the saddler's on his errand for Mary. Bold Street was one of the principal streets of Thanshope, and close to the very shop to which Myles was going was a place known to the vulgar as 'th' Club.' This was a billiard and whist club,

frequented by the golden youth of the promising town of Thanshope.

It was a spot not exactly loved of the
mammas of the said town, and much discussed by the young ladies of the same.
Much iniquity was vaguely supposed to be
perpetrated there : some of the piously disposed spoke of it as a 'den;' others, who
knew nothing, and wished to appear as if
they knew a great deal, said it was 'as bad
as the worst of London clubs,' which remark
may serve as a specimen of the mighty self-
consciousness of little provincial towns—and
'den' is a word which has about it a fine
abstract flavour of awfulness.

It is probable that, as a matter of fact,
much bad whist was played there ; billiard
balls were knocked up and down, and bets
made ; too much spirits were probably con-
sumed ; as many dull, coarse, or vulgar tales
were told, as much aimless scandal was
talked, as many praiseworthy efforts were
made to ape the manners and tone of metro-

politan clubs, as in most provincial institutions of a similar kind.

Myles went to the saddler's, which was next door to this temple of hilarity, fashion, and fastness; got the straps which Mary had spoken of, and then came out to take his way to the town-hall. As he passed the portico of the club, he saw just within it a back which he remembered, clothed in broadcloth. Beside this figure was another, that of a mere lad, with a babyish face and no chin to speak of, who would have been better in the cricket-field, or even grinding at his Latin grammar. On his small-featured, insignificant face was stamped an expression of foolish glee and admiration.

The first individual was speaking; Myles, strolling leisurely past, heard the words, in the loud, strident voice :

'Such a chase, my boy! but I succeeded. I found out where she lives, and waylaid her; gave her my protection whether she liked it or not. Unless I'm much mistaken, we shall soon be very good friends. She's a deep one—those demure things always are. Ha, ha !'

' I say, Spenceley——'

' Doosid pretty, though. D——d good eyes she has, and knows how to use them. Look here ! do you want your revenge for Saturday night ?'

' Oh, yes ! Come along !'

They walked forward to the interior of the hall, and were lost to view.

Never before had Myles felt the singular sensation which just then clutched him—a kind of tingling, half of rage, half of shame, from head to foot—a tempest of his whole mental being. He was in a white heat of fury, and only two ideas were distinct in his mind : to find Adrienne, and to punish her insulter.

Almost unknowing how, he hurried to the town-hall, up the stairs, through the library, into the reading-room. Would she be there ? Yes, she was there, in her usual place. He strode towards her. She was not even pretending to read or write. She sat pale as ashes, and trembling, as he saw in his approach.

'Miss Blisset!' he almost whispered, as he went up to her, and bent over her, his face dark with suppressed indignation, his eyes aflame. If she too had not been moved out of all conventional calm, she must have started at the expression which flashed from his face upon hers.

'Oh, Mr. Heywood, will you be so very good as to go home with me now, at once? I have been so frightened and—insulted!'

Her voice broke, though her eyes flashed. How proud a front soever she might have showed to her insulter, the reaction had set in : the remembrance was not to be borne unmoved.

'I know you have,' said he, in a low, emphatic voice; and a tremor shook him too as he looked at her, and saw how beautiful she was. He had admired her as she sat in repose, but now every fibre of his nature bowed to her, and he felt a passionate desire to do something, anything, which should set him apart in her eyes from others. Yet, after his first swift glance, he scarcely looked at her, and said very little. Words appeared weak and trivial—he could not express in them his detestation of the conduct of that other man, or how profoundly he reverenced her.

'How was it?' he asked, speaking composedly, but clenching his hands, and crushing together what he held in them.

'It was that man,' said she, in a low, breathless voice, 'that hideous man. I don't know where he saw me. I think he must have followed me, but when I got to that little lane, he suddenly overtook me, and spoke to me. I could not turn back. It would have been much farther—and so lonely. I did not answer him; I went on very fast, but he detained me so long in that lane—he would not let me pass. I thought

I should—bah! I thought, when we got into the town, that he would have left me, but he did not. He came to the very door of this place, and I dare not go out for fear he should be there yet. Oh, I am so glad to see you! I thought you were never coming.'

She had leaned her head upon her hand, or she must have seen the light that flashed suddenly into his eyes—not the light that had been there at first. He drew a long breath, but succeeded in not betraying for a second his emotion, as she turned, pale and quivering with excitement, and put her two little slender hands upon his, saying earnestly:

'You have been very kind to me. What should I have done if you had not helped me?'

'It has been a pleasure to serve you,' he said constrainedly. 'Do you feel fit to walk home now?'

'Oh, quite!' she answered, picking up

10—2

her note-book, and they went away together.

Myles walked with her to the gate of her
uncle's house, and said, as they paused
there :

'Of course you will never come again, Miss
Blisset ?'

'Never. Of course not.'

'Then—then.—' he faltered, unable to say
what he wished.

'But I shall see you again, of course,' said
Adrienne quickly. 'You will come again.
My uncle wishes you to come again. And
you will—yes ?'

'You are sure it wouldn't be an intrusion ?'
said Myles doubtfully.

'Very far from an intrusion,' she answered.
'You will be welcome—and you will be expected until you come.'

With which, and with a warm hand-shake,
she disappeared.

Myles did not pause to-night, to contem-
plate the street, or to look out for the light

in the window. He took the shortest and straightest course into the town again, went direct to Bold Street, and stopped before the club.

There was a light in the vestibule of that building, and a waiter stood at the door surveying the passers-by, and feeling no doubt that he looked negatively fascinating.

'Is Mr. Frederick Spenceley here?' inquired Myles, quietly and politely.

'Mr. Frederick Spenceley?' repeated the waiter, while an expression of ill-humour crossed his face. 'I rather think he is, and in a deuce of a temper too. If Mr. Frederick Spenceley keeps on coming here, I shan't stay. Well, do you want to see him?'

'I should like just to speak to him,' said Myles, ever calmly and politely; his one object being to penetrate to Mr. Spenceley's presence, content to pocket his burning fury until he was face to face with him.

Mr. Spenceley evidently enjoyed little

favour in the eyes of the waiter, or the latter would hardly have allowed a working-man to penetrate into that *sanctum sanctorum*, the billiard-room.   As it was, he said :

'Well, if you go straight ahead upstairs, you'll find him in the billiard-room, I expect. But perhaps you want to see him down here ?'

'Oh, no !   I can go to him.   Upstairs, you say ?'

The waiter nodded ; and Myles, obeying his direction, found himself on the first landing, opposite a door inscribed 'Billiards.'

He knocked, but no reply was given, which was accounted for by the loud and overpowering voice of Frederick Spenceley, whose accents drowned all other sounds.

Myles opened the door, and walked into the room, which was like most other billiard-rooms ; four green-shaded lights above the table ; the marker standing in his place, look-

ing sulky—he too having received his share
of the compliments of Mr. Spenceley that
evening.

(It was a significant fact, that not one of
Frederick Spenceley's inferiors would have
felt anything but pleasure in his degradation
or humiliation.)

There was Charlie Saunders, the insignifi-
cant-looking boy, whose pretty pink-and-
white face was now a good deal flushed, and
who laughed foolishly now and then in his
high-pitched voice. Opposite, with his burly
back towards the door, was Frederick Spenceley, shouting very loudly, and freely expres-
sing his opinion that the cloth was a confounded bad one, and that the table was not
level.

' It's your eye that's not level, Freddy, my
boy,' said his youthful opponent; ' and
your cue too. Look out what you're
doing.'

' D—n it! it isn't. Where's the cha-alk?
It's my beastly luck,' roared Spenceley,

against whom the balls had broken most unfavourably the whole evening.

Had the fellow been in the least intoxicated, Myles would have retired; but he was merely noisy and ill-tempered, and accordingly the workman chose that moment to step forward and touch Mr. Spenceley on the shoulder.

With a violent start, which contrasted somewhat curiously with his previous bluster, he turned; and when he saw Myles, his face assumed a deep hue of anger, and perhaps of some less noble feeling.

'I want a word with you,' said Myles curtly; and young Saunders paused to stare at the new-comer, while the marker turned and looked on too.

Be it observed that neither of these men loved Frederick Spenceley. A billiard-marker, however, is not always in a position to resent affronts, and Charlie Saunders was a person of less importance than Spenceley, whatever might be his private opinion of him. Moreover, the whole proceeding took them by surprise, or — perhaps they might have interfered.

'If you like to come to another room, where we can be alone,' pursued Myles composedly, 'lead the way. I don't care where it is.'

'What the —— do you want, you ——?' growled Spenceley, recovering his pluck, or what he was pleased to consider his pluck.

'I think you remember me. I don't need to introduce myself,' said Myles. 'Now look here! You've been behaving like a black-guard again—perhaps you can't help that— but, in any case, you'll be pleased to take your attentions to some other quarter than that one. You know what I mean.'

'I'll be—' (a volley of the dash dialect) 'if I do, you fool! Be off, and don't annoy gen-tlemen. Clear out, I say, or I'll call the waiter, and have you kicked out.'

There was that in Myles's face, so far removed from brutal violence, which was con-spicuous in every word and gesture of Spenceley, that the others were quiescent. How he had got there was a mystery to them; but being there, they were Englishmen enough to wish for fair play, and had sufficient sense to perceive that the workman was no blackguard, whatever his interlocutor might be.

'You were in Markham's Lane to-night,' went on Myles composedly, though his face had become white, and his lips were set.

'What's that to you? What business have you to come spying on gentlemen?'

'If I were you, I wouldn't say too much about spying. You know what happened there—in Markham's Lane, I mean. If anything like it happens again—just once again——'

He paused.

'Well?' said Spenceley, with a sneer and a taunt, 'what will be the consequences, my fine fellow?'

'They will be unpleasant to you, for

I'll thrash you within an inch of your life.'

'Ha! ha! *ha!*' roared Mr. Spenceley, but somehow there was a false note in the full chord : it failed of rounded, complete harmony.

'Freddy, what have you been up to?' cried Charlie Saunders, in amaze ; but he did not ask what the other man had been 'up to.' It appeared to be taken for granted that he had good ground for his complaint.

'Look here, you beggar,' observed Spenceley to Myles ; 'just get out of this, before you are turned out, and don't interfere in things you don't understand.'

'I go when I have your promise to behave yourself in future—not before.'

'Wha-at? Promises? I don't make promises to cads.'

'Then I suppose you've never promised yourself what you deserve. I'm waiting for a promise to me, not a cad, and I'll stay till I get it.'

'D—n you! will you be off?' shouted Spenceley, in a sudden passion, as he saw the cool, scornful face of Myles, and his eyes contemptuously measuring him from head to foot; and took in with a side-glance the scarcely concealed smile upon the faces of the others. 'Will neither of you fellows ring the bell, and have this fool turned out?'

The rules of the club not providing for such an emergency, they took no notice of what he blustered at them, while Myles replied coolly as ever:

'When I've got what I want, I'll be off, as I said.'

'Perhaps you want to keep the little darling to yourself,' began Spenceley.

'Drop that!' said Myles sharply, for the first time losing his perfect self-command.

'Ah, that's it! We don't want to be disturbed in our little game. We are so very industrious and literary in our pursuits——'

In clenching his hand, Myles felt something in it which he had forgotten—the
parcel containing Mary's straps. The paper
which enwrapped them had got loose.
One strap had fallen coiling upon the floor;
one remained in his hand. He looked
at it, and felt very strong to wield it. He
turned once more to Spenceley, saying :

'Do you promise never to speak to, or
molest the lady again ?'

'Make promises to *you*, about that little
jade . . . .' began Spenceley jeeringly, but
he did not finish the sentence.

Myles's hand, like an iron vice, was at his
throat, and during the paralysing astonishment and bewilderment of the other two,
Frederick Spenceley received such a thrashing as he had many a time deserved, but
which circumstances had hitherto denied to
him. Myles's hold, strengthened by a passion which lent him irresistible power, did
not for one moment relax. At last Saunders
turned and rang the bell, but not before

the fine broadcloth coat was in ribbons upon its owner's back, and the face above it purple and almost suffocating, did Myles fling him away from him, remarking coolly :

'Perhaps that will answer as well as a promise. If ever it's necessary, there's the same thing, and worse, ready for you a second time.'

He turned to find the door open, and the waiter staring in, aghast.

'Kick him out! Fetch some water!' cried young Saunders, bending over the prostrate figure of his friend. 'Kick him out, I say!' he reiterated. He was remarkably small and slender in figure, and doubtless felt that it would be a mockery to attempt the deed himself.

Myles turned towards the waiter, who still blocked up the doorway.

'Well,' said he tranquilly, 'I am waiting; which are you going to do? Kick me out— or let me pass?'

The billiard-marker had made no attempt

to interfere. The insults received that very evening from Spenceley rankled in his mind; he was well-pleased at the humiliation of the bully. The little waiter looked up for a moment at the tall, muscular, sinewy young man who towered above him, with a pale face, and a look of inflexible determination and power about his eyes and mouth, and a frown of anger, terrible in its intensity, on his brow. He stood aside silently. Myles turned and said :

' If I'm wanted again about this business, my name is Heywood, and I live on the Townfield. I can easily be found.'

No answer was returned : he composedly picked up his second strap and walked away.

CHAPTER VIII.

AFTER-THOUGHTS.

'WHAT ails thee, Myles?' asked his sister, as he came into the kitchen.

'Me? Nothing, lass. Here's your straps. The new one has had a kind of inauguration, but I reckon it will have done it good more likely than harm.'

'What dost mean?' she asked, staring at him.

'Oh, nothing!' said he with a slight laugh, as he leaned against the mantelpiece with his arms folded behind him, his favourite attitude.

'Hast changed my book, Myles?' inquired
Edmund.

'Eh, I clean forgot it,' replied Myles,
with a start. 'I'm very sorry. Fact is, I
was called off, and I never thought of the
book again.'

'Well, it doesn't matter,' answered Edmund, who was in high good humour at his
mother's absence.

Mary also seemed less constrained, though
nothing would have induced her to own that
she was glad her mother had left them. She
moved about more freely, and as she passed
to and fro, 'putting things to rights,' she
was heard to sing snatches of no less a song
of praise than the 'Old Hundredth.' And
when her household work was done (for
Myles's adventure had not taken long, and it
was now barely eight o'clock) she brought
her work, and sat down with her brothers;
and though there were shadows brooding
over them all—darker shadows, and deeper,

than they imagined—they formed a very happy trio.

Mary especially felt happy and contented. She was devoted to her brothers—loved Edmund with a mother's and a sister's love combined, while she looked upon Myles as her ideal of all that was good and manly. He had given her no cause to think other-wise. With regard to her own merits, she was humble; but let any one impeach in the slightest degree those of Myles or Edmund, and she became fierce, proud, and resentful. Something in Myles's mien to-night disturbed her, she knew not why.

'Wilt have thi pipe, lad? It's theer; I'st get it in a minute.'

'No thank you, Molly. I don't care about smoking to-night.'

'Did iver ony one see sich a chap?' said Mary, secretly filled with pride in him. 'He ne'er drinks, and he ne'er hardly smokes, and he ne'er does nowt disagree-able.

'He hasn't a redeeming vice,' said Myles ironically, watching her fingers as she plied her needle, and forcing himself to speak, though he did it half mechanically. What was she making?' he asked.

'A shirt.'

'For whom?'

'Why, for thee, lad!' said Mary, with a laugh and a look at him; and Myles returned the look with a smile, and instantly became lost in a long train of reflection.

Edmund and Mary loved him, and looked up to him as to a superior being, as the centre figure in their lives, and the person around whom clustered their hopes, fears, and loves. Beyond them, out of their circle, was Adrienne Blisset; was it in the nature of things that she could ever behold him with eyes like theirs? No, never; because she was instructed, and they were ignorant. Well, was adoration the best thing for a man? Was it not better to adore? Could there be any shame in the worship of a

woman like Adrienne ? He decided, no. It
was not the giving up of independence—it
was the bending to a superior being which,
when that attitude was self-elected, was the
highest independence. Here all was secure,
safe, assured. Nothing would ever change
the love of these two for him : outside there,
where Adrienne was, all was stormy, cloudy,
feverish, uncertain : he knew not what she
thought of him—what feelings or no-feelings
her gracious manner might cover.

He had defended her—from the first moment of their intercourse his attitude had
been made by circumstances a protecting
one : he felt at once an inferiority and a
superiority to her, which two things do
surely form part of the primal basis of pure
and holy love. He stood still, leaning
against the chimney-piece, thinking of what
he had this night done for her sake, and his
face flushed at the remembrance.

'Can she ever be like another woman to
me ?' he thought. 'It is impossible. If it

were possible I should be a clod.' For what he had done counted for something with Myles : he was not one of those heroes who will thrash you half a dozen fellows, twice as big as themselves, and then require to be reminded of such a trifle.

He was not quite sure, even now, that he felt unmixed satisfaction in the deed. To thrash a cowardly bully, who seemed unable to express himself without the assistance of copious volleys of oaths, was one thing, and Myles contemplated with some complacency the fact that he had done it. But if any evil consequences should ensue to Adrienne !

After a moment he reassured himself. He did not believe that Spenceley knew her name. He had not mentioned it. Myles would have died rather than utter it himself in that company—that would indeed have been a casting of pearls before swine, of which he was naturally incapable.

If Mr. Spenceley chose to prosecute him

he would own himself guilty, and take his punishment—anything rather than drag her name into the discussion; but he doubted much whether Spenceley would wish to draw public attention so pointedly to the fact that he had been flogged by a workman in the billiard-room of his own club. That would have been to expose his own brutal insolence and violence, and to hint, moreover, at some discreditable deed in the background which had called forth the attack. Myles began to wonder how that beautiful sister of his, whom he had spoken to that morning—could it be that morning?—would receive her brother. Then his thoughts wandered off again to Adrienne.

'At any rate, I can't face her yet. I must stay quiet awhile until it has blown over. Perhaps, as she's so very quiet and goes out so little, she'll not hear about it; and then I could call, and not mention it, and it would all pass over.'

A knock at the back-door roused him.

Mary lifted her head, and cried, 'Come in !' but after a pause the knock was renewed.

'It's Harry,' observed Edmund. 'Thou mun open to him, Myles, or he'll go on knocking for half an hour.'

'Ay, poor lad, I suppose he will,' said Myles, going towards the door, while Mary maintained absolute silence, continuing her work.

Myles soon returned, accompanied by a young man, slight and somewhat delicate-looking, pale-faced and fair-complexioned, whose calm, open countenance was pleasant to look upon, despite a certain vagueness in its expression—-not a want of intelligence, or anything approaching vacancy, but rather as if something escaped him and left him apart from other people.

'Good-evenin', Mary—evenin', Ned,' he said, in the very softest and gentlest of voices.

'Sit down, Harry, and have supper with

us,' said Myles; and when he spoke Harry
Ashworth's infirmity became apparent.

Myles had to go close up to him and
speak, not very loudly, but very slowly and
clearly. He was almost deaf, in consequence
of a fever he had had when a boy of twelve.
He was twenty-five now, and the weakness
increased each year ; it was probable that in
a few more years he would be stone-deaf.
He was a frequent visitor at the Heywoods',
and a great friend of Myles and Edmund ;
Mary and he had little to say to each other
beyond the words of greeting and farewell.

There was a certain constraint this evening immediately after his entrance, on account
of what had happened in regard to Mrs.
Heywood, but this constraint was dissipated
by Harry himself.

'I hear your mother has gone,' he remarked.

Myles assented in a grave sort of way.

Mary's cheeks flushed, and she did not
raise her eyes from her work.

'She thinks of being married soon, then?'

'I expect so,' said Myles.

'Ah,' said Harry; and then, without any embarrassment, changed the subject.

'We may expect changes soon, Myles, I reckon.'

'What changes?' asked Myles, who had come close to Harry, while the latter had placed his chair close to Edmund's sofa.

'The master's coming back—so I hear.'

'Oh, him!' said Myles, again trying to turn up his nose, and again failing to do so.

Harry laughed, and Mary remarked:

'Eh, but I could like to see yon chap. He mun be some and clever.'

'Molly thinks he must be clever,' said Myles to Harry, who nodded.

'I don't see why he shouldn't be, choose how. I think you're a bit hard on him, Myles. We know no harm on him.'

'Yes, we do. We know he's neglected his business and his property. He's six and twenty if he's a day, and he's never looked in upon us since he came into possession. He's a gawmless chap—he must be.'

'Well, we'st see that when he comes. Have you heard as Mr. Lippincott, his health's failin', and he's ordered abroad ? They say he can't live.'

Mr. Lippincott was the sitting member for Thanshope.

'Nay, I heard nothing of that,' said Myles reflectively. 'Then, suppose he dies, we shall have a fresh election.'

'Ay ; and I have heard,' pursued Harry, not without a twinkle of humour in his eyes, 'as it's possible Mr. Mallory may stand, if Mr. Lippincott resigns or dies.'

'What !' ejaculated Myles. 'And who is to oppose him ?'

'Spenceley—Bargaining Jack.'

'Why, Myles, thou'd be hard set to know who to vote for,' said Mary innocently.

Myles suddenly recovered his presence of mind, and shouted to Harry :

'You've heard wrong, lad. Mallorys are all Tories, and always have been—it's bred in the bone; and Bargaining Jack reckons to be a Conservative too, so far as he's anything. Conservatives manage better than us. They would never run two candidates in Thanshope—in fact, they only run one for the look of the thing. They can't get the wedge in here.'

'Well, I have heard too,' continued Harry, 'as how Mallory is a Radical—a Liberal, choose how.'

'That I'll never believe till I hear him say it himself,' said Myles decidedly. 'And from all I've heard, I think you've been misinformed, Harry.'

'Well, perhaps I have,' said Harry peaceably. 'It doesn't matter to me which way it is.'

Nor did the others appear to take much interest in the subject, for it dropped, and Mary began to get supper ready.

At that meal the conversation was carried

on almost entirely between Harry and Myles. Harry was a spinner, in receipt of a large wage. He was, as has been said, a pleasant, comely-looking young man, and if not very robust, did not look unhealthy. Many of his friends wondered why he did not marry ; for he was turned twenty-five. He and Myles and Mary Heywood were beginning to be looked upon as drifting into the old-maid and bachelor ranks.

At all times, early—terribly early—marriages are the rule in Lancashire ; but in those halcyon years of plenty and golden prosperity preceding the American Civil War, they had been more numerous than ever.

After supper, Edmund, stretching out his arms, said in a muffled kind of voice :

'Eh, I say, it is some and hot here. I wonder what it's like outside.'

'Why, the air's pleasant enough on the Townfield,' said Harry.

'I could like to feel it,' remarked Edmund. 'I've not been out these three days.'

'Well, come along and take a turn,' said Myles good-naturedly, well knowing that Edmund's motive for suggesting such a thing at that time was that the dusk was rapidly gathering : there were fewer people about, and he was less likely to be observed.

Edmund jumped at the offer, and Myles, giving him his cap, and taking his own, drew his brother's arm through his, shouting to Harry :

'Wilt come with us, or wilt stay with Molly ?'

'I'st stay and have a pipe till you come in, if Mary's no objection,' said Harry ; and Mary, by way of answer, pointed to a china basket on the mantelpiece, in which stood half-a-dozen neatly-made ' spills.'

These spills were a mystery to the household. Mary gave it out that she liked to have them. They looked tidy like, and did for lighting the pipes ; but it was a well-known fact that Edmund did not smoke at all ; that Myles preferred to light his pipe with a coal or a match, and that the only visitor who enjoyed the privilege of smoking in that kitchen was Harry Ashworth. Yet no one ever suggested that the lighters were kept in stock for Harry's benefit, though Edmund had been perilously near doing so once or twice. Had he or any one else uttered that theory, it is impossible to imagine what Mary would have said—possibly nothing at all, for she was, in practice at least, a strong upholder of the theory that 'silence is golden.'

The two brothers went out, leaving the door open, and a waft of the somewhat cooler outside air penetrated to the kitchen. The gas was not lighted; the fire had burnt low; the room was almost dark. Mary could no longer see to work, and sat, with her head thrown a little backwards, in the high-backed, red-cushioned rocking-chair. The clock ticked: everything was very still. It was Harry who spoke first, in his soft voice.

'Warm and close, this here weather, Mary.'

'Ay,' said Mary; ''tis.'

'How does Ned get on?' he asked; for though she did not speak very loudly, she spoke deliberately, and he appeared to hear her easily.

'He feels th' heat aboon a bit,' replied Mary.

'Ay! I dare say.'

A pause, while Harry puffed away at his pipe, and Mary offered no further observations on men or things.

'I took a long walk o' Sunday—yesterday,' observed Harry at last.

'Did yo? Where to?'

'Reet o'er th' moors to th' top o' Black-rigg.'

'It's to' far. Thou'rt none strong eno' for sich like walks.'

'Yea, but I am. I set me down on th' heather, and listened wi' all my might, and I thowt I heard a bird singing.'

'Happen a lark?' said Mary, after a perceptible pause.

'Happen. I should ha' gone to church in th' evenin', but I can't hear—nowt distinct, that's to say—and I'm a'most inclined to think that I didn't *hear* yon lark, but only thowt I did, from memory, thou known.'

'Ay,' assented Mary.

'And when I go into church, and hear th' organ buzzin', and th' voices all mixed up wi' it, and can't make out what it is, it fair moithers me; same as when I look up, and see th' parson speakin', and don't know what it's about.'

'Ay,' said Mary, laconically as ever, but this time there was the faintest possible vibration in her voice.

And there was another long pause, while Mary's eyelids drooped. He did not see that—it was too dark; and had he seen it, he could not have known that those eyelids were sore with repressed tears, which burnt them, and which she would not allow to flow.

' Sometimes,' his voice broke in again, ' I get discontented. I'm main fond o' music, as you know, Mary.'

' Ay, I know thou art.'

' And it troubles me above a bit sometimes as I should be deaf, for it just takes away my greatest pleasure. Sometimes I wish I'd been blind instead.'

No answer from Mary, till Harry, in a hesitating voice, said :

' What dost think, Mary ? Is it very wrong to have such thoughts ?'

' No, I dunnot,' replied Mary. ' I call it very nateral. If I was deaf, I reckon I should make more noise about it than you do. I wonder what them chaps is doin'. It's time they was comin' in.'

' Don't thou go out. I'll find 'em, and tell 'em, for I mun be goin' too,' said Harry, rising.

Mary had begun to poke the fire violently, and now let the poker fall with a loud rattle, as Harry, without her knowing it, had advanced close to her, so that her elbow struck against his outstretched hand.

'Dule tak' th' fire-irons!' said she impatiently. 'I conna think what ails 'em. Good-neet to you, if you mun be going,' she added, shaking hands with him, and, as soon as he was gone, lighting the gas.

Presently her brother came in. The house was locked up. Mary went to bed, followed by Edmund. Myles was left by the dying-out kitchen fire, with a book on the table, which he never opened, but sat till far into the night, living through some of those strange hours of still, silent, yet vivid, rushing, mental life which come to all of us sometimes in our youth, and which are like no other hours in our experience.

CHAPTER IX.

A TEA-PARTY.

' Mir war's so wohl, so weh !'

AFTER that evening, Myles found himself in a position which he at least found full of difficulties. Two things happened, both of which he had looked upon as probable ; the news of what had happened spread, and Frederick Spenceley did not prosecute. The waiter who had allowed Myles to go into the billiard-room was dismissed ; the billiard-marker who had stood by shared the same fate.

It would be difficult to guess what object, real or supposed, was gained by this measure ;

but it seemed to afford great satisfaction to many minds. Spenceley found it convenient to leave home for some weeks, and Myles heard no more of his share in the transaction.

There were endless tales in circulation— the facts, the names, the causes of the affair, all got mixed up in the wildest and most inextricable confusion, as in such cases they always do. The principals maintained absolute silence, and let report work what wonders it would or could.

> 'Bear not false witness; let the lie
> Have time on its own wings to fly!'

They adhered to the precept, and the result was that they and their grievances were soon completely obscured in the buzz of talk, conjecture, wrong guesses, and wild surmises which. gathered about them like a thick cloud. One thing soon became apparent; and, once secure of that, Myles cared nothing for the rest. Adrienne's name was not known. The cause of the *fracas* was generally supposed to be a woman; but the

tale which gained the greatest favour was
one taking the side of the workman—that
mysterious 'workman,' whose name had
somehow disappeared in the midst of con-
tradictory reports, and whom no one could
distinctly specify, because there were so
many workmen in Thanshope. How was a
genteel person to know one linen jacket, or
its wearer, from another? This report, which
preserved a kind of likeness amidst all its
variations, was to the effect that Frederick
Spenceley had deserved his thrashing; for
that he had been taking undue liberties with
the young man's sweetheart—and her name
was Sally Rogers, was Frances Alice Ker-
shaw, and she was a dressmaker, was a mill
hand, and lived in half a dozen places, and
worked in as many factories, quite certainly
and positively; she was very pretty, and he
was very jealous; or, she was not a particularly good-looking girl, but Fred Spenceley had had words with the young man
before, and had wished to insult him.

Myles maintained a rigid silence upon the subject, even when Mary came in one day in a state of unusual excitement, exclaiming :

' Eh ! Ned Myles, have ye heerd tell o' what's happened ?'

' What ?'

' Jack Spenceley's lad has had such a leathering,' said Mary ; and told the rest of it with much excitement and volubility, for her.

Edmund manifested a lively interest in the story, and Myles admitted indifferently that he had heard something about it.

They were, however, not much given to gossiping at that house, and the subject soon dropped.

Then came Myles's other difficulty. He did not know whether boldly to go and call at Mr. Blisset's as he longed and desired to do, or whether to remain away. He plagued himself with wondering what she thought about it, and then tried to believe that she had perhaps not even heard of it—her life was so very retired, she saw and heard so little of what was going on outside. Then he might go? But suppose she did know, and he appeared as if he came to be thanked and made a hero of? He contradicted himself ten times a day; decided to go—to stay —to go—and stayed because he absolutely could not decide which was best.

So the days went on until Saturday, and he had not had a glimpse of her—only the remembrance of her grateful eyes and the pressure of her hand, as she bade him good-bye at her uncle's gate before *it* had all happened. When Saturday afternoon came, his longing to see her was growing almost unbearable, and he had the sensation that if he went out of the house, his feet would turn mechanically towards Blake Street.

❋   ❋   ❋   ❋   ❋

It was Saturday afternoon; the clock-hands pointed to five; Mary's ' cleaning ' was over, and the house was quiet. Edmund lay upon his sofa with a headache,

and Myles was softly reading to him, glad
of some monotonous occupation which should
divert his thoughts somewhat from the topic
which at present tyrannised over them.

Edmund had been reading in a magazine
about the works of the Brontë sisters, and
Myles had procured him ' Jane Eyre ' and
' Wuthering Heights ' from the free library.
' Wuthering Heights' lay as yet untouched :
it had not yet laid its strong and dreadful
spell on the boy's spirit. They were deep in
' Jane Eyre.' It proved a spell which caused
Edmund to forget his headache, and en-
chained the attention of Myles himself, with
its passionate expression of the equality of
soul and soul, and its eager conviction of the
supremacy of mind over the differences of
rank or place. Its burning radicalism went
straight to Myles's soul, while its deep
poetry touched Edmund's inmost heart.

At this moment they were wandering
with ' Jane ' over the summer moors, home-
less, friendless, foodless, penniless ; and they

had forgotten all outside things with her, as she reposed herself beneath the broad sky, on the friendly bosom of her mother— Nature.

'Hist!' said Edmund suddenly, 'there's a knock.'

Myles paused. Some one knocked at the front door. Mary had heard it, and rose from her rocking-chair.

'Thee go on wi' thi' readin',' said she, going out; and they heard her open the door, and a low voice—a woman's voice—ask her some question.

With an inarticulate exclamation, Myles half rose, the book open in his hand, and as Edmund was in the act of inquiring what was the matter, Mary came in again, looking rather bewildered, and saying, as she turned to some one who followed her :

'Myles, here's a lady wants to speak to thee.'

'Why did you not come?' said Adrienne, going straight up to Myles. 'Why have you never been to see me? I have waited and waited, until I could wait no longer.'

He stood, crimson, unable to speak a word, but looking at her with eyes that must have told their tale—which must have warned her had she been less excited and earnest.

'How could you go and do a thing like that, and then never take any further notice of me?' she continued. 'I have thought of nothing else since I heard of it. It was most wonderfully foolish—oh, very foolish; but oh, I do thank you, and honour you for it, with all my heart. It is exactly what such *canaille* deserve, and it was nobly done —it was indeed!'

'Miss Blisset . . . you . . . you—It was nothing. Any one would have done it. I couldn't have rested or slept till I had punished him. I was obliged to do it.'

'Ah, that is how *you* put it, no doubt—but any one would not have felt so—only you would. I can never thank you—never.'

'Well, don't then! I—it makes me

ashamed of myself—it does indeed,' said he earnestly.

'But whativer is it o' about, miss?' said Mary, putting into words her own and Edmund's boundless astonishment.

'Is it possible,' said Adrienne, turning with wide-open eyes to Myles—'Is it possible that you have never told them? Did he not tell you?'

'Nay, he's ne'er told us nowt,' said Mary.

'I never heard of anything so extraordinary,' said Adrienne, with still a vibration in her voice, which showed how much she was moved. 'You must have heard about that man—Spenceley—who insulted me, and . . ."

'Thank heaven, your name has never been uttered,' interposed Myles hastily.

'And your brother, who had once before sent him away when he tried to annoy me, at the library, went to make him promise to behave himself, and he would not. Was not that it? So he flogged him.'

'Eh—Myles!' said Mary, with a long-drawn intonation, compounded of incredulity, pride, and pleasure. 'Eh—h—Myles! I niver did—no niver!'

'So it were you, Myles,' said Edmund. 'Thou hast kept some and quiet about it. But I'm glad thou did it.'

'And he has never come near my home— never given me a chance of thanking him,' pursued Adrienne. 'You must understand, now, why I have come.'

'Ay, I can so,' said Mary, regarding her with great favour and cordiality, for this praise of Myles touched her to the very heart. 'Won't you sit down?' she added.

'I don't wish to disturb you,' said Adrienne, hesitating.

'Eh, no sich thing. Sit you down,' said Mary, drawing up the rocking-chair, in which Adrienne sat down, and Myles stood leaning against one end of the mantelpiece, feeling the need of a support of some kind; for he felt a sort of intoxication and a bewilderment, and a strange, subtle, new life in the very fact of Adrienne's presence.

'I had to inquire where you lived,' she said, looking up at him. 'You did not even tell me that. You once mentioned that you lived on the Townfield, and I thought I should never find your house; but the first person I met told me where you lived. But would you never have come?'

'I—I hardly liked to come. I did not know whether you might have been—displeased, perhaps,' he said, with some embarrassment.

'My uncle has often asked when you were coming. He wants to see you again. But now you will come soon—yes?'

'I—yes. I should like to,' said he.

'I hope you don't mind my coming here,' said Adrienne to Mary.

'Eh, no! Lord, no!' said Mary earnestly. 'I'm reet glad to see you. Yon chap would ne'er ha' told us what he'd been doin'. He's so—stupid.'

'Yes—so I should think,' said Adrienne, meeting Mary's eyes with a smile.

And then looking at Edmund, she said,

'I've heard of you, too. You are not strong.'

'No,' said Mary, answering for him. 'He's ne'er one o' th' strongest, and to-day he's getten a headache.'

'Don't you do anything for your head-aches?'

'Nay, I just bide 'em out.'

'That is a pity. I could do something for them—if I come again, I will bring you some-thing that will do them good.'

She went on talking to Mary and Edmund, who seemed to feel no embarrassment in the intercourse. Adrienne certainly possessed in a high degree the art of putting people at their ease in her company. Mary and Edmund were not usually communicative in first interviews with strangers; but this stranger appeared to take their hearts by storm, and quickly succeeded in making them

forget that there was any difference in station
between them. She apologised for her intrusion much more particularly than she
would have done to a woman whose servant
had opened the door, taken her card, and
announced her with a flourish. This demeanour was not put on—it was her natural,
spontaneous manner, springing from instinc-
tive politeness and geniality of nature.
Everything about her was true and pure
—what Myles was accustomed to call in
the vernacular, 'jannock.' Mary, also, was
nothing if not jannock ; and the two girls—
the lady and the factory-worker, seemed
instinctively to get on.

'I must not detain you any longer now,'
said Adrienne, at last. 'I see you are going
to have your tea. But I should like to know
you. Would you mind if I came again,
now and then ?'

'Eh, I'st be vary glad,' said Mary, 'if so
be we're not too simple and plain like for
you. Yo'seen we're nobbut working folk . . .'

'Well, I am a working person too, and like seeks like,' said Adrienne.

'I reckon you're a different mak' o' worker fro' us,' said Mary.

'I am sure I work as hard as you at least, and am as tired and as glad of rest as you, when my work is done.'

'You look tired now,' said Mary, fixing her large, clear eyes upon Adrienne's pale and somewhat weary face, from which the glow had faded. 'Where do you live?'

'Up at Stonegate, in Blake Street.'

'My certy! But that's a good step!' said Mary, who, like many of her class, was nothing of a walker. 'We're just goin' to have our tay — won't you draw up and have a sup, and a bit o' summat to eyt?'

That homely, cordial Lancashire invitation, 'Come and have a sup, and a bit o' summat to eat'—what Lancashire ears are there that do not know it and love it for the kind thoughts it arouses! It went straight home to our lonely Adrienne : a mist rushed over her eyes ; she said somewhat hesitatingly :

'Oh, I should like it. You are very kind, but I fear——' she half turned to Myles.

'Myles, coom out o' yon corner, and behave thisel', mon! Thou can when thou's a mind to,' said Mary briskly. 'Now draw up,' she added to Adrienne. 'Tak' off your hat, and I'st hang it up, so! And Myles'll see you home. He's got nowt to do toneet.'

Mary must have been inspired when she made this suggestion.

'Oh, I need not trouble him now,' said Adrienne, with a radiant smile upon the approaching Myles—'unless he has forgotten the way to my uncle's house, as I begin to think.'

'It's much better I should go with you. It's Saturday evening,' said Myles, seating himself beside her, and throwing a fleeting glance towards her face.

She was content, pleased, even flattered at the friendly way in which she had been received. Her expression said that as plainly as words could do. Myles began to lose some of his bewilderment, and to gain somewhat more confidence.

'Eh, I've forgotten th' mowffins!' said Mary suddenly, a shade crossing her face. 'We mun really wait while I toast th' mowffins.'

She jumped up and produced tea-cakes out of a cupboard, and Myles suggested that perhaps it did not matter about the muffins. Mary was, however, firm, and bade him cut some bread-and-butter while she toasted.

'And mind thou cuts it nice and thin, and not all i' lumps,' she added in admonitory tones.

Myles, much too simple-minded to see anything derogatory in cutting bread-and-butter, began, but in half a minute Adrienne had jumped up and laid hold of the knife.

'Stop! That is clearly not your sphere,' said she, laughing into his embarrassed, yet ever-attractive face. 'It is not stern enough —not commanding enough. Let me do it.'

Unaware of the distinguished example set by the Wetzlar heroine in the bread-and-butter-cutting line, Myles watched the deft fingers of his enchantress as if no woman had ever been known to cut bread-and-butter properly before.

Mary, who grew visibly and every moment more satisfied with her guest, toasted the 'mowffins,' buttered them, and tea was proclaimed ready with acclamation.

Then Edmund came to the table; they all sat there, and Mary made tea in state, apologising for not having the best tea-things because of the impromptu nature of the visit.

'I am sure these seem delightful tea-things,' said Adrienne, smiling.

The festivity was altogether successful as regarded Adrienne, Mary, and Edmund. But Miss Blisset cast every now and then fleeting glances at Myles, and was not quite at her ease about him, for he alone of all the party was silent and grave. It was the deep intensity of the delight within him that caused this, but Adrienne could not be supposed to know that—in very truth, as yet she honestly believed the greater admiration and liking to be on her side. That delusion was soon to be ended, but at present she was under its influence.

The meal was not long over when she said she must go, and promising Mary to come again, she went away, accompanied by Myles.

Their way lay through what was called 'the Park.' They turned in at the large iron gates of a town pleasure-ground, laid out in gravel walks, grass plots, seats, and flower-beds. They were on a height. The town lay below, with the gilded spire of the town-hall cleaving the air, and the hazy-looking blue wall of Blackrigg to the north and north-west.

As they walked slowly along a broad terrace, unoccupied save by themselves, Adrienne asked, in her quick, foreign way :

' Say to me, Mr. Heywood—you are vexed that I came ?'

' I—vexed—nay !' was all that he could say.

The current which for the last week had ever been hurrying more and more quickly forward, had now arrived at the verge. It leapt over it in a bound, and carried everything before it. He was madly in love, and all he could do was to. say as little, be as brief as possible, for fear of showing her, startling her, perhaps repelling her ; for he was intensely conscious of the difference ; all his dearly-loved, passionately-cherished theories of equality could not blind him to the fact that they were not equals—that while he loved her with a strength that shook his nature with its power, yet the bare thought of touching her, holding her hand, speaking to her on easy and familiar terms, came to him with a sense of impropriety— brought him the conviction, *non sum dignus.*

'You were so quiet,' said she. 'You would hardly speak to me. I was afraid I had offended you.'

'Not at all,' said poor Myles, unable to say more lest he should say too much.

'I am sure,' pursued Adrienne, stopping in her walk and looking earnestly at him, —'I am sure you know that I did not mean to offend you ; and you could not be so hard as to wish me to keep silence. You behaved splendidly. I felt that I must thank you for it.'

It was growing too much for him to stand there quiescent, and hear that voice, which contained all melody for him, and to see that face, those eyes, looking at him so. The eagerness of desperate love came storming down upon prudence, and hurrying words of devotion to his lips. Mastering himself by a strong effort, and clasping, or rather clenching his hands behind him, he said, in what seemed to Adrienne a singularly calm, colourless voice :

'You make too much of it. I would rather not be thanked for it.'

'You are hard upon me to say that. It gives me such pleasure to thank you, but you deserve at my hands that I should comply with your wishes—after what you have done for me. But you cannot guess what a delightful feeling it is to one so lonely as I, to suddenly discover that there is some one who has been not afraid to stand up for her—and to some purpose.

'I should have thought you would have many friends,' remarked Myles, endeavouring to change the too-fascinating subject.

'I—no indeed. I don't think any one with fewer friends ever lived.'

'But you may have left friends behind you on the Continent ?'

A momentary pause while he looked at her. It was as though some sudden blow had struck the words back from her lips to her heart—then she said steadily :

'Some few ; but chiefly benefactors rather than friends—benefactors who befriended and helped me in my loneliness and destitution, for my father and I were sometimes almost destitute.

'Destitute ?' echoed Myles, shocked.

'Oh yes ! I have not always lived in Lancashire, you know. No one seems to be poor here. I have known what it is to look at a piece of money worth sixpence, and know that if I spent that upon my supper I should not have a penny in the morning to buy breakfast with.'

'But not seriously ?'

'I assure you it seemed very serious to me. I have sunk lower. I have known what it was to go supperless to bed, wondering what poor little trinket or book I could spare in order to get a breakfast next morning.'

Myles was silent, and Adrienne continued :

' That, you know, is not what is considered respectable for a young lady.'

' Hang respectability !' was all he said.

' Not at all ! I like it. After all the fever and the turmoils, and the ups and downs, and dreadful uncertainties of that life, my present one is like Paradise. Oh, rest is a very sweet thing—rest and security, and a strong arm to help you.' (Myles turned to her with parted lips.) ' Your home is beautiful. That sister of yours is so calm and good. I love her already. She must be very dear to you.'

' Ay, I love Mary dearly.'

' Yes. Both she and you, and all of you, look as if you had had a home all your lives. Do you think I might go to see them again ?'

' They'll be only too glad. I never thought you could sympathise so much— with our sort,' said Myles constrainedly.

' To-morrow you will come to Stonegate, will you not ? and then I will tell you my story, and you will perhaps understand how it is that I sympathise with "your sort," as you call it, and why I think so much of what you have done for me.'

'I will come, with pleasure.'

'To-morrow afternoon, then, I shall expect you.'

They walked the rest of the way in silence, and Myles left her at the gate.

CHAPTER X.

'DEEPER AND DEEPER STILL.'

IT was a lovely Sunday afternoon on which Myles took his way to Stonegate. He found Adrienne alone. She said her uncle was taking his afternoon airing in his bath-chair in the garden, and did not wish to be disturbed; his old servant, Brandon, was with him.

'But sit down,' she continued, 'and we can have a talk.'

With that she picked up her knitting and began to work.

'You will talk,' said Myles, 'if you keep

your promise. You promised to tell me about yourself.'

'Do you really want to hear that?'

'I came on purpose.'

'Well, I will tell it you, and I hope it will have the effect I intend.'

'What effect is that?'

'You are determined to look upon me (I have seen it, so don't be at the trouble of denying it) as something fine and delicate, and unused to roughness and hardship.'

'Yes, one can see plainly enough that you are that.'

'Can one? Well, I'll begin my story, and you shall learn how appearances may deceive.'

Adrienne related well. She did not exaggerate; there was nothing strained—no striving after effect; but there was colour, pathos, life, in her tale, and a subtle poetry thrown over all, by her way of looking at things.

Myles, in listening, felt as if he were

actually wandering with her on that nomadic
life she spoke of; through the great foreign
capitals, and the country villages, and the
towns, big and little; to be sojourning with
her in the gay, feverish watering-places; to
survey the distant, rose-tinted Alps. He
utterly forgot where he was, and knew only
her and her life.

There had been two brothers, she told
him, of whom her father was the youngest
and her uncle the elder. Kith and kin they
had none, and their patrimony was small.
Both were gifted, but in different ways.
Adrian, her father, was artist to the marrow
of his bones. Richard, her uncle, had also
some taste for art, but more of the analytical
and critical than of the synthetic description;
he had been, moreover, at one time a practical man of business, and had made money
—he was not rich, but thoroughly indepen-
dent. Her father had had the gift of spending, not of making. The brothers had
parted early. Adrian, as soon as he was

his own master, had said farewell to home, and had gone, first to Germany, there to study the music which his soul loved, and which had beautified his otherwise weary, disappointed life.

Some time was spent in Germany; then two or three years in miscellaneous and somewhat aimless travel; then back again to Germany, to music, and to love. The fair, clever, and penniless daughter of a poor professor and man of science won his heart, as he hers, and they married.

With marriage came the feeling of an insufficiency of means, and the desire to augment them led him into business speculations of a nature which he did not in the least understand: the bubble burst, and Adrian Blisset found himself a ruined man in less than a year after his marriage. Adrienne's mother died at her birth; the girl had never known that holy bond, however much she might have longed for it. Her father chose to lay part of the cause of his wife's death to the

anxiety induced by his extravagance and folly
—moreover, he had adored her—and from the
hour of her death he had been a changed
man. He had his own living and that of
his child to gain, but he settled nowhere.
His life became nomadic. He and the little
one did not sojourn long in the tents of any
particular tribe. Scarce a city or a town of
any importance in Europe, but had sheltered
the unconscious head of the infant, or been
trodden by the child's uncertain feet, or by
the sedate step of the maiden, careworn
before her time, while she knew intimately
many an out-of-the-way nook, unnamed by
Murray, Bradshaw, or Baedeker, amongst
Italian hills, deep in the sunny lands of
France; Thüringian woods and slopes, or
sleepy red-roofed Rhenish hamlets.

A restless ghost drove the musician with
his child and his violin hither and thither,
never permitting him to stay long in any one
place and gather substance ; but ever, so soon
as the novelty had worn off, seeming to drive

him forth on a fresh search after—what? Adrienne had learnt at an early age to ask herself that question, and sorrowfully to give up the answer.

Sometimes he was in funds, when he showered all kinds of presents upon her, and called her his dear child, his *Herzallerliebste;* but oftener they were plunged in poverty, sore, sordid, dreadful poverty. His moods varied distressingly, from kindness that had in it something fitful and sinister, up to the dark and melancholy silence which was his most frequent humour. He was proud, and his pride was of a touchy and intractable kind ; it offended men of business, and estranged friends and pupils.

Adrienne had had many teachers and many strange lessons, and the whole had combined into a varied and truly most unconventional education. Her father had lavished musical training upon her. At Florence, where they stayed a whole year, longer than anywhere else, she had wandered about with a kind-hearted old artist, who led her about with him to the great galleries, and showed her the grandest pictures, and made her know the beautiful buildings, till she had imbibed the undying loveliness of such masterpieces as Giotto's Campanile, or Michael Angelo's Duomo, and had discovered that her favourite thing in Florence was the 'Pensiero' Medici of the last-named artist.

'You remind me of him,' she added, suddenly looking at Myles. And she had sat, at thirteen years of age, for a picture of 'Gravity.'

'Was that what he called you?' asked Myles.

'Yes. Gravity, or Sedateness was his name for me—and it suited me.'

She had had to part from her good old friend, and that had cost her the pain which parting brings to those who know they will not meet again.

In Paris, Adrienne had had lessons in

democracy from a young universal genius, whose talents were too vast to stoop to any ordinary walk of life. He lived in a garret, and planned schemes of a perfect republic. Adrienne had not felt much grief on parting from him.

A monstrous learned professor, who lived at Bonn, in a *Schlafrock*, slippers, and spectacles, had taught her a little store of Greek and Latin. But her greatest teacher had been a strange, absent-looking professor, in Berlin—a man of literature and philosophy, who had been very fond of her, and had given her freely of his very best. Her uncle, Mr. Blisset, looked upon this as a providential circumstance, for he found when she came to him, that he had no tyro to deal with, but one already instructed in philosophy and its terminology.

Two years ago her father had died; and just before his death, she had learnt for the first time, that they possessed any relation in the world. She had received a letter to give to her uncle. She fulfilled the behest, and that was how she first met Mr. Blisset.

'And what did he say? How did he receive you?' asked Myles eagerly.

'I was chilled,' said she, 'as I sat opposite to him and saw his pale, impassive face, and watched how he raised his eyes now and then from that letter. He gave me no reply that night; told me nothing; did not intimate whether he were pleased or displeased to see me, but ordered a room to be prepared for me; and the next day he told me that my father had asked him in his letter to give me a shelter until I was able to find some employment by which I could support myself. My uncle said that if I could endure to live buried alive with an old man, and work hard at a sedentary employment, he would give me a home and pay me a certain sum every year. I accepted his proposal 'gratefully, and have never repented it; and I trust he never will, either.'

There spoke the true Adrienne Blisset.

'And you are happy here?'

'As happy as I expect to be. It is a great thing not to be miserable.'

'That's what our rulers appear to think we working-men ought to feel,' said Myles sardonically, his thoughts for the moment flying off at a tangent.

'Are you bitter against your rulers?' asked Adrienne tranquilly.

'I am bitter against some of them—a pampered set of rich men, who never had a care in their lives, but don't mind how many other people have to bear. There are some, now—Bright, and Cobden, and the like—for them I'd die. There's that in their faces which says they have not a mean thought, nor a desire but for our good; but the most of them'—he shrugged his shoulders—'those lily-handed politicians who call themselves Radicals in these days, and plan how to prevent a working-man from getting his beer, but have half-a-dozen sorts of wine at their own tables, and go mincing about at public meetings, talking lightly of trials that would make them cringe if they had to face them; talking about "supply and demand," and how to improve the condition of the lower orders —isn't that the phrase? Much they know about the lower orders, and how to improve them! They don't know what ails them yet.'

He laughed sarcastically.

'It is true, they are a somewhat emasculate type,' said she; 'but I don't see what right you have to blame them much. It is the working-man's own fault that they can do no more for him.'

'His own fault!' he echoed incredulously.

'Now don't eat me up, please! I wonder if you and I differ essentially in first principles on this subject. You have thought about it, haven't you?'

'Ay, I have. I've plenty of reason to think about it, when I see such fellows as Frederick Spenceley and young Mallory living on the fat of the land, without having lifted a finger to get it, or proved by a single act that they merited it.'

'Mr. Mallory,' said Adrienne slowly, 'you say you have seen him; has he come home?'

'No. I meant to speak figuratively. I don't see him; but I know it is so. If I don't know him, I know the likes of him——'

'But—but what about him?' she asked, still with the same slowness and a kind of hesitation. 'What has he done wrong?'

'He has done nothing; that's what he has done wrong,' said Myles. 'Well, he's coming home soon; we shall see how he breasts the storm—for we are in for a storm, sooner or later. But don't you think, Miss Blisset, it must make a man think to see these contrasts—a man who has the least bit of a power of thought?'

'No doubt. And what conclusion have you come to in the matter?'

'The conclusion that it's a crying injustice.'

'To whom?'

'To—well, to put it broadly, we'll say to the working-man—but I mean to those in general, who work very hard, and get very little.'

'In what way?'

'Miss Blisset! Where is the justice of fellows like that having that money without either rhyme or reason; and of fellows like——'

'You,' suggested Adrienne demurely.

'I don't mean me in particular, but my class in general, earning from thirty to sixty shillings a week—the very best paid of us— in payment for hours and hours of close, hard work.'

'I suppose it is not the work you object to?'

'No. I like work. I should be lost without my work.'

'The property which those young men enjoy has been earned with trouble as great, or probably, from an intellectual point of view, greater than your weekly wages.'

'But not by them.'

'Suppose it had been earned by you, and you wished to leave it to your only son, whom you had educated with a view to his inheriting it, and the law stepped in and said you should not, but should leave it amongst a number of working-people whom you had never seen or heard of—how would you like that?'

'But that is an exaggerated view of the case.'

'I don't see it. I don't believe you have ever considered the subject fairly. And answer me this : Suppose the average working-man became possessed of that money, or of part of it—*money which he had not earned* —money which had become his by a lucky chance : do you think his use of it would be worse, or as good as, or better, than the use made of it by those two of whom we are speaking ? Do you think it would do him a real and permanent good : increase his self-respect, lessen his self-indulgence, make him

steadier, soberer, more inwardly dignified,
worthy, and honourable ?'

She was looking earnestly at him, and
Myles frowned, the words driven back from
his lips. Did he know one man amongst
his fellow-workmen, on whom the possession
of such money would have such an effect ?
Would it have such an effect upon himself ?
The generalities of the writers who cried up
the working-man and his wrongs seemed
suddenly to grow small, and to shrink into
the background.

'Oh,' went on Adrienne, 'I don't think
you working-men know in the least how
noble your work intrinsically is. You only
see that others are outwardly better off than
you, and you clamorously demand a share of
that wealth. You don't see how disastrous
to your best interests such an acquisition
would be.'

Myles had started up, feeling terribly
humiliated.

'You think so ill of us !' he exclaimed.

'You could come and see us yesterday, and talk to my sister as if she had been your sister—and now you reproach us in this way. Good-bye !'

'Stop !' said she, laying her hand upon his arm, and looking earnestly into his face. 'How wild and impatient you are ! Think a moment ! It is not of *you* I am speaking. Do you know any other working-man to whom I could speak in this way ?'

She paused. It was true ! Perhaps Harry Ashworth might hear those words and bear them—he knew of no other who would do so ; and while he was stung and tortured by what she said, he felt a bitter consciousness that it was true. But he stood still, and waited to hear the end.

'I am speaking to you with a purpose,' Adrienne went on in the same tone, low and quiet, but full of vehemence. 'Since that night when you stepped forward in my defence, I have thought much about you—very much. I have studied you, and you do not know how well-used I am to studying people. The more I have studied you, the more I have felt that you were both generous and high-minded—and terribly hot-tempered,' she added, with a smile, which Myles thought must have charmed the temper of a ravening wolf. 'Just think what you, a workman, might do, by setting an example to your fellow-workmen. Take the right side. You are too good for the commonplace career of an ordinary " intelligent working-man," for a blind submission to trade-union rules, and for an obstinate resistance to your masters, just because they are your masters, or because your union bids you resist them. Don't be a tool; use your reason; consider the why and wherefore of things. Be answerable to your conscience alone for all you say and do. Help to show your fellows that all improvement in their condition must arise actively from within, not be received passively from without—you know that, and own it, don't you ?'

'Yes,' said Myles quickly, folding his
arms and leaning against the mantelpiece,
his eyes fixed upon her, as she stood before
him, with her head a little thrown back; her
eyes alight, looking beautiful in her energy
and excitement.

'I wish,' she said, 'I often wish that I
were a working-woman, like your sister. I
would show you what I meant; how toil
could be ennobled.'

She paused. Myles's heart was beating
wildly. Something, whether God or devil
he had no time to think, hurried quick words
from his lips; in a voice as low, as vehement
as her own had been, he said:

'Do you? And suppose it ever came to
the point? Suppose some day some working-
man came to you, and told you he loved you;
that he could see how toil might be ennobled,
if you would help him to do it—there would
be an end of your philosophy. You would
think of the cottage to live in, the floors to
scrub, the rough neighbours, the coarse com-

mon life, the children to tend, and make, and
mend, and sew for ; and if you could get over
that, there would be the man himself—a great
rough fellow—a workman, not a gentleman,
a man of rough speech, like—like our sort.
You would have to work for him, too ; to
cook, and sew, and wash for him ; to obey
him—*you.* When he said " Do this," you
must do it, and when he called " Come here!"
you must go to him.   That's the way amongst
us working people.   What about the ennobling of toil *then ?*'

He spoke jeeringly, and hated himself for
doing so ; and listened for her answer in a
state of wild, if silent, excitement.

Her hands had dropped, her eyes had sunk,
her face was burning ; she turned away. If
he could have trusted himself to move or
speak, he would have fallen upon his knees,
and begged her pardon.

' Oh, Myles !' said she, at last, in a very
low voice. He bit his lip till the blood came,
at that sound ; the most maddening, in its

mingled sweetness and bitterness, he had ever heard. 'I suppose I gave you the right to say that,' she said, 'and to demand an answer too. You put it tersely, certainly. As you speak, I can see the very life rising before me that you picture.'

'And yourself in it !' said he, still with a sneer, though he would have given the world to ask her to forgive him.

'No. You forget something,' she replied, walking to the window, while he still leaned against the mantelpiece. 'You made it all hard and sordid. You forgot the very " ennobling " that began the discussion. I *could* fancy myself in such a home—a working-man's wife—but to become that, I must love that man ; and in the life you described there was no love. The man I loved, be he workman or prince, must be a gentleman—not a brute.'

'Ah ! and supposing you met this working-man—or whoever he might be ?' suggested Myles, in a calm, restrained kind of voice.

' If I met him, and if I loved him, and he loved me, and asked me to marry him, I would say " yes ;" and I would love him, and serve him faithfully to the end of my life.'

The words fell softly and gently, almost timorously, as if she hesitated to speak of such a thing ; and yet with a certain gentle firmness which said that they were no sentimental verbiage, but expressed the steadfast feeling of a steadfast heart. But each word was like a drop of liquid fire in the young man's veins. She seemed suddenly to be close beside him—a possibility, a thing he might dream of—and fifty thousand times higher and farther off, and more impossible to him than ever. How could *he* ever hope to bend that heart to love him ? The very thought was insanity.

He mastered his emotion, and walked up to her. She turned, but did not look at him.

' I beg your pardon, most humbly,' said he.

' It is granted freely. I dare say it has

been good for me ; it has reduced my vague theories to the language of common sense. I had no right to reproach you with the faults of your class, and expect nothing but milk and honey from your lips in return. We understand each other. Oh, but yours is a biting tongue ! It cuts like a knife.'

'It forgot itself when it turned against *you.* But, remember, your words had roused me. You made me blush for my own " vague theories," as you call them. If you could not have said what you did, to any other work-man, do you suppose I could have spoken so to any other young lady ?'

'No, no. I suppose not,' said she, but her face was still downcast. The glance which he at last received wavered almost timidly. She resumed her seat and her work, saying : 'And you will think of what I have said ?'

'I will—seriously. I believe you are right, but the thing was too wonderful for me. I could not attain unto it—all at once.'

The conversation was turned, as if by one

consent, to books. Adrienne's heart was beating unwontedly fast; her knight had not only surprised, but somewhat subdued her; delighting her at the same time. He was no tool; he could turn upon her, and he had the front of a ruler. That glance and that voice were not to be forgotten. She thrilled as she remembered them. She was glad he had not gone; the sensation that he was still there was pleasurable, with a strange potency of strength.

The door opened, and Mr. Blisset was wheeled in, and a servant brought afternoon tea. Then Mr. Blisset began to talk, and Myles to listen. Mr. Blisset had some of his niece's conversational power. The time flew insensibly, till supper was announced. Myles rose, fearing he had intruded too long.

'No,' said Mr. Blisset. 'Stay, unless you are tired, and my niece will give us some music.'

He looked at her, and she said, 'Yes, do stay?' And Myles stayed.

That evening Adrienne sang some songs.
She finished with ‘ *Neue Liebe, neues Leben,*’
and Myles went home with its last passionate words ringing in his ears :

‘ *Liebe, Liebe, lass’ mich los !*’

Would it ever ‘let him loose,’ that love which
had sprung up so suddenly and so strongly,
making every other feeling weak in the glow
of its might and strength ?

CHAPTER XI.

PROMISES.

THAT visit was but the first of a long series. Mr. Blisset was pleased to see the young man who listened so patiently and so deferentially to him ; and Myles had an ever-growing conviction that Mr. Blisset's views of men and things, of right and wrong, were deeper and sounder than his own ; riper, truer, and more justly balanced. Myles learnt much in these visits and conversations.

Adrienne had been many times to the cottage on the Townfield, and had completely won the hearts of Mary and Edmund. She had opened up a new field of delight and wonder to the boy, by putting him in the way of studying botany, and his enthusiasm knew no bounds. She lent him books and specimens, and Harry Ashworth, who was a great walker, brought him all kinds of plants, and ferns, and mosses, from the moors on which he was wont to spend his Saturday afternoons and Sunday mornings.

When Myles and Adrienne were in his house at the same time, they seemed to have little to say to each other; which was, perhaps, not surprising, for their subjects were not those discussed by Mary and Edmund. Harry Ashworth had a great deal to ask Miss Blisset about music; she comforted him too, for she helped him to some scientific understanding of the mighty harmonies of which he was fast losing the outward apprehension. Harry had not read much about music or musicians; he had, while his hearing had been pretty good, contented himself with drinking in the sounds themselves. Adrienne soon discovered that the sorrow of his life was his failing hearing, and one evening it occurred to her to tell him the story of Beethoven. Mary and Harry and she happened to be alone. Adrienne began, and related that saddest of stories. It had the effect she intended.

Harry sat with one hand shading his face, in an attitude which he had assumed soon after she began the story, when she said : 'And at last he wrote to one of his friends and confessed that he was growing quite deaf—that if he went to the opera, he must sit close to the orchestra, and even then, even leaning over towards it, he could scarcely hear.'

Mary went on knitting. Adrienne's voice, somewhat raised, slow, distinct, and clear, told the tale of that mighty genius—Christ-like in the immensity of his woe, and the utterness of his separation from those around him. She went through it all. She told

him about the great symphonies, about
Beethoven's one or two sad, luckless love-
episodes; his poverty; his love for the thank-
less young profligate, his nephew; the per-
formance of the Choral Symphony—of that
great adagio 'in which we discern the slowly-
stalking movement of a god!'

'When it was over,' Adrienne went on,
'the audience were almost mad with rapture
and delight, and the applause was deafening
—thundering—it resounded through and
through the great room! the master still
stood with his bâton in his hand, his back
to the audience, till one of the vocalists
gently turned him round, and he saw them
all—how they were wild with pleasure and
emotion; *he* had thus moved them by his
heavenly music to "joy," and he had heard
no sound of it all.'

She paused. It was the life which she
most loved in all truth or poetry; to her
Beethoven's sufferings were as actual as his
genius or his grandeur.

She saw Harry look at her with an expression which told her that he too understood, and she went on to the end—told of the bitter loneliness of those last years, that death in harmony with the life—that passing away of the Titan soul in the sublime music of the spring thunderstorm, and then she was silent.

Harry looked at her for a moment, started up, and took her hand.

'Thank you, miss,' said he, and left the house.

'Eh, Miss Blisset,' said Mary, wiping her eyes, 'you're like no one else as ivver I heerd tell on afore. You've done a kindness to yon poor lad, such as he never had yet.'

'I'm very glad if you think so.'

'Yo've gien him summat to console him. He'll go about now, thinking he may bear his deafness quite easy like, seein' yon man as yo' towd us on were so great and patient. His mind is fair beautiful—Harry's mind is,' said Mary, moved out of all reticence.

'I like him very much,' said Adrienne;
'very much indeed.'

'Ay! He's good—good to th' marrow of
his bones, he is.'

'Like you, Mary. You and he are well-
matched.'

'Eh, nay! Eh, don't think o' that! He's
ne'er said nowt about it.'

'He will, sometime!'

Mary was silent, with a downcast face, till
at last she said:

'I know you'll ne'er say a word to no one
about it. I can trust you to tell you this, as
whether he ever says owt about it or not, the
vary thowt of ony other mon than him fair
gives me a turn.'

'Yes,' said Adrienne. 'And you do deserve to be happy, Mary. I wonder how it
is that you and all yours are so different
from other people. I always feel well and
happy, and right with the world when I am
with you.'

Later, as Myles walked with her up Blake

Street, Adrienne remarked that the end of September was approaching and the evenings darkened earlier.

'Yes,' said Myles, 'soon winter will be here. And then . . . . now then, you,' he added, to a passer-by, who gave Adrienne a very close berth ; 'mind your manners when you're passing a lady.'

'I didn't know you had lady-friends, Myles Heywood,' replied a smooth voice, as the offender paused, and looked at them.

'Oh, it's you !' said Myles, with trenchant contempt. 'If I'd known, I wouldn't have troubled to speak to you.' And he passed on.

'Who is the man ?' asked Adrienne.

'He's my—-step-father,' said Myles, in a peculiar voice. Adrienne had heard the whole story from Mary ; Myles had never been able to speak of it.

'Oh, forgive me for saying it, but I wish you had not spoken to him in that way.'

'Why ? How ?' he stammered.

'Has he ever done you any harm?'

'Not directly; but I can't abide the very looks of him.'

'There!' said she, with a somewhat nervous smile; 'you are too contemptuous. Reverence is better than contempt; it is indeed.'

'Reverence? Would you have me reverence *him?*'

'Yes. You ought to reverence human nature—your own nature—in him. If you could have heard yourself speak! Do you know what you would do, if any one spoke to you in that way?'

'What?'

'Why, you would—I think you would shake him. I can just see you make one stride towards him, and fasten upon him—poor fellow!—to teach him manners.'

'You mean that I have none myself. Well, you may be right.'

'Are you offended?'

'Miss Blisset—you could not offend me.'

'I think I could. But do think of what I have said; and try not to be so contemptuous. Will you?'

'The next time I meet Jim Hoyle, I'll take off my hat to him politely—since you wish it.'

'You will drive me to despair! How different you are from your reasonable sister, who sees the right bearings of things at once; and from your sensitive brother, who . . . .'

'Yes, Ned is like a girl for delicacy,' said Myles, a sarcastic flavour in his voice. 'Well Miss Blisset, I will try hard to please you. Next week there's a fellow coming that I *have* a contempt for, if I ever had for any one.'

'Who may that be?'

'Mr. Sebastian Mallory, our so-called *master*.'

A pause. Then a hesitating, 'In-deed!' from her, the intonation of which Myles did not remark.

'So I'll try to be polite to him, if our paths cross—which I hope they won't.'

'Perhaps they may not. But now do try,' said she. 'You may find it easier than you think.'

They parted at the wicket, and Myles went home, to find Edmund gone to bed, and to sit up himself, reading 'My Beautiful Lady,' which Adrienne had lent to Edmund, never supposing that Myles would look at it, or that he would take any interst in it if he did. But he pored over it, and his heart-strings trembled to the poet's notes : it was he himself, his own thoughts put into poetry, as the lover waited his lady's coming. And as for the end, Myles read it differently ; to please himself, he allowed common sense to step in—Adrienne was not consumptive.

CHAPTER XII.

MR. MALLORY'S POLITICS.

'*Philinte.* Mais on entend les gens au moins sans se fâcher.
Alceste. Moi, je veux me fâcher, et ne veux point en-
   tendre.'

Le Misanthrope.

DURING the following forenoon, Myles sat alone in the outer office, employed exactly as he had been on the day of Mrs. Mallory's visit, weeks before. Wilson was going his usual round in the works, and Mr. Sutcliffe, the manager, was out.

Pausing at the end of a column of figures, he raised his eyes and saw coming down the street something which caused him to open his eyes in surprise, though surprise was not his usual expression.

It was a very high and very swell phaeton, with a pair of magnificent bays, which danced along the street, as if its shabby, clog-worn stones caused much distress to their aristocratic hoofs. The driver of this (in Thanshope) unique conveyance was a young man in light grey clothes and a round cloth cap—no English cap : indeed there was, at least to the uninitiated Thanshope eye, something un-English in his whole appearance. He was, however, master of his cattle, as even Myles could see. Beside him sat a slight, dark boy, with a plain, queer, but attractive face; and behind was a very correct-looking groom.

'Who on earth is that chap?' was Myles's first very natural thought, as he forgot his work, and gazed in the blissfulness of ignorance at the vision. The next moment he could have bitten off his tongue could he have had the feeling that he had not bestowed a second glance upon the whole affair, for the dancing bays came sidling down the street, and the driver pulled them up before that very office door; moreover, he had caught sight of Myles staring at him, and had given him in return a lazy look from a pair of rather sleepy eyes.

Now Myles knew it was the 'so-called master'—it was Sebastian Mallory: a second glance at the fair, though bronzed face, the yellow hair and moustache, the proudly cut features, and the indifferent expression, displayed sufficient likeness to his mother to make the first intuitive conviction a certainty.

Furious with himself at having been caught staring openly and wonderingly, Myles forgot his voluntary promise to Adrienne, and, in order to prove that, whatever his open eyes might at first have seemed to intimate, yet that he was not really at all struck by anything he had seen, he turned his back to the door, and was apparently bending with the deepest attention over his work, when that door was opened; he heard a voice conclude some injunctions to the groom, and the answer which followed:

'*Jawohl, mein Herr.*'

'Foreign servants, even!' murmured Myles, shrugging his shoulders.

'Good-morning, my good man,' was the next thing he heard, in an accent as different from that of the Thanshope 'gentleman,' as Adrienne's was different from that of the Thanshope lady.

He turned round and looked up; he was forced to do so now, and without noticing the lad who stood in the background, he faced Mallory. The two young men confronted each other for the first time.

So far as expression and complexion went, they were as great a contrast as could be imagined. Both were tall, spare, and well-built, and there the resemblance ended. Myles was, as has been said, quick, passion-ate, lithe, alert, with a temper that sprang into action on every possible occasion, with eyes that flashed, brows that contracted, very often in the course of a day. Sebastian Mallory was graceful, but there was some languor, real or assumed, in the grace. He was handsome, but the good looks were certainly marred by the bored expression on his pale, fine features. His eyes moved slowly; they were very good eyes, luminous, and hazel in colour, but they did not look as if they would easily flash. He spoke, looked, moved, as if he found life rather troublesome, and scarcely worth the trouble when it had been taken. He had taken off his cap when he entered the office—foreign fashion, and Myles saw that his face, all save the forehead, was somewhat bronzed; but it was with the bronze of a hot 'sun—not nature, naturally he was pale. His hair, too, seemed to have caught the sun at the ends, elsewhere it was just yellow hair. Every gesture and movement was full of the polished ease of high cultivation.

Myles, looking straight at him, said to

himself, ' One of your languid, heavy swells are we? I'm afraid we shall ruffle his fine feathers in this horrid democratic place.'

He had Mrs. Mallory in his mind's eye, as he surveyed her son: her principles were well known—the divine right of kings—the Conservative side through thick and thin, good report and evil report; Church and Constitution intact through every storm; our greatest Premier, the late lamented Duke of Wellington; *the working-man in his proper place* (wherever that may be); rich and poor, gentle and simple, a providential arrangement which it would be sinful and impious to think of disturbing.

Thinking of all this, Myles surveyed Sebastian Mallory, and as he found him entirely different from any young man he had ever seen before, and as most of the Thanshope people, great and small, were of the Radical persuasion, he immediately concluded that he was right—what had been bred in the bone must come out in the flesh, and it was quite clear that Mr. Mallory was a Conservative of the bluest dye.

Meanwhile Sebastian had been looking at Myles, too, surprised at receiving no answer to his remark, and still more surprised to observe that the eyes of the 'good man' were fixed intently, criticisingly, and with an unabashed steadfastness upon himself, and appeared to measure him over from head to foot, in a manner which was, to say the least, singular. The cap of the young man remained on his head; he did not rise; he did not ask what he could do, nor the visitor's business; he simply looked at him with a pair of remarkably keen, piercing dark eyes, and Sebastian returned the look, until at last a gleam of amusement appeared in his sleepy eyes.

That look of amusement was not lost upon Myles; it irritated and angered him. He was so terribly in earnest about all he did, thought, or believed, as not readily to see the comic side of a question, while it was

Mallory's chief foible to take everything in this world that came to him as rather amusing —if not too troublesome.

'*Ma foi!*' he observed, with a quaint look, but very good-naturedly; 'they told me in the train that I should be surprised at the Thanshope people, and so I am!'

'Perhaps they'll be equally surprised with you,' said Myles concisely.

'Well, they may,' replied Sebastian, coolly. 'Do you know who I am?'

Myles hesitated a moment, much wishing to say, 'No, I don't,' but integrity got the upper hand; he only put the fact as disagreeably as he could.

'I should suppose you are Mrs. Mallory's son.'

Sebastian turned to the brown-faced, dark-eyed boy who stood behind, and remarked smilingly:

'You see, *I* am nobody, Hugo; only my mother's son; and yet here I am upon my own property.'

The youth nodded, and glanced thought-
fully at Myles, who could not resist going on
with the rather perilous game he was playing,
and who remarked dryly :

'You'll find that we count a good deal by
residence and relationship here.'

'So!' said Sebastian, with the amused,
half-smile still playing about his lips and in
his eyes, to the intense exasperation of Myles,
who naturally saw nothing at all to laugh at
in the situation. There was something, too,
about Mallory which struck a subtle blow at
his pride and self-esteem—something which
in his innermost heart he knew to be superior
to himself, though he passionately refused to
admit the idea.

'Your guess is correct,' went on Sebastian.
'I am Mrs. Mallory's son. And now I should
be glad to know who and what you are—one
of my work-people, perhaps ?'

The young man did not seem to be at all
annoyed at what was taking place ; indeed,
there was that in his manner which said that

he was mildly amused with the whole affair.
He looked around as he spoke, with a lazy,
criticising glance, but it was the glance, as
Myles keenly felt, of a master, and of one
who was accustomed to be a master. He
was surveying his property, and question-
ing one of his servants. All the revolu-
tionary element in that servant was in per-
turbation.

'What am I?' he began, when Sebastian,
who had taken off his cap on entering the
office, said suggestively :

'Hadn't you better take your cap off?'

'That is a matter of opinion,' said Myles,
the blood rushing to his face. 'It is not the
fashion here. As for me, I doff to no man,
and but few women.'

'Ah! well, we won't quarrel about it.
As you say, it is a matter of opinion,' said
Sebastian politely ; but there was something
in the tone which made Myles feel small, and
as if he had been behaving childishly—not a
comforting feeling.

'But I interrupted you,' continued Mallory, who seemed to be acquiring gradually a sort of interest in the conversation; 'you were going to tell me who you are?'

'My name is Myles Heywood, and my business is cut-looking and part of the over-looking in this factory,' said Myles.

'Heywood,' repeated Sebastian, his eyes losing their lazy look, 'Heywood; where have I—ah, yes! A cut-looker—I don't know what that is.'

'Likely enough not,' said Myles.

'But it is quite certain that I must learn it,' pursued Sebastian; 'what is it, if I may ask?'

An uncomfortable sense began to steal over Myles, that Mr. Mallory was courtesy itself, and that too, under considerable provo-cation. He gave a short sketch of his busi-ness.

'Thanks,' said Sebastian. 'And now— by-the-bye, I am absolutely forgetting my business—is Mr. Sutcliffe in?'

'Not now ; he will be in about an hour.'

'In an hour ?   Then I must go over the works without him.   Is there any one here who knows all about it—you, perhaps ?' he added quickly, as if struck by a happy thought.

The idea of leading Mr. Mallory round the works excited the liveliest aversion in Myles's mind.

'Wilson, the head-overlooker, is above me. He generally does that,' said he.

'Wilson—I ought to remember Wilson. He has been here a long time, hasn't he ?'

'He has,' said Myles, rather emphatically.

'I thought so.   Well, where is he ?'

Myles, despite himself, very much despite himself, felt the influence of Sebastian's manner.   He would have been glad could he reasonably have classed him with Frederick Spenceley, but no such classification was for a moment possible.   He wished he had not made that difficulty about going through the works. He suddenly remembered his voluntary promise to Adrienne, and felt that he could not tell her he had kept his word. But too proud, or perhaps too shy, to suddenly change his manner, he said, in the same curt tone :

'He's going round the works. If you'll wait a minute I'll send him to you.'

'Thank you,' said Mr. Mallory.

Myles went out of the office, and across the yard to the factory ; and Mallory, putting his hand upon Hugo's shoulder, silently pointed to the workman's figure, and they watched him until he had gone into the mill.

'Hugo, you have not a good ear for English names yet, but I have. I have heard that man's name just lately—yesterday, in fact, in the train as we came from Manchester. He is a fellow I must know something more about. Did you notice him ? He has a splendid face.'

'Splendid manners too, I think,' said the boy sarcastically.

'Yes,' replied Sebastian meditatively. 'Heywood! If he had not mentioned his name when he did, I think I should have lost my temper. As it is, I shall try another plan. There he goes! What a row comes from behind that door!'

Then they looked through the window.

'What a prospect!' said Sebastian, glancing over the head of his companion, who leaned with both arms on the window-sill. 'This time last week, do you remember? we were with—ah, what was their name—those girls and their brother?'

'On the Luzern steamer, going to Fluelen,' said Hugo, his eyes fixed upon the dead wall opposite.

'Just so! Do you remember the sunset, and Mount Pilatus, as we came back? Well, Pilatus is there now—and we are here.'

Hugo made no answer, but Sebastian saw a smile curve his cheek.

'Why, you might be pleased rather than not,' said he.

'I am not displeased,' replied the lad, with the same little smile.

'Not displeased that I took a notion about duty into my head, and whirled you away from Switzerland, and snow-peaks, and Alpine colouring, to Thanshope, Hugo?'

'Suppose you had obeyed the call of duty without whirling me away—had left me behind somewhere?' said Hugo tranquilly.

'Ah, so! That is at the root of it,' said Sebastian, laughing. 'What an odd——ah, here comes the overlooker! Now, Hugo, observe me doing the merchant-prince, and prepare your artist-eye for some shocks during the progress we are going to make.'

Wilson entered in a state of high excitement.

'Mr. Mallory, sir, this *is* a hunexpected pleasure! I couldn't believe it. 'Ow are you, sir? Well, I 'ope. We've looked forward long to this event.'

'Very well, thank you. I found myself at home sooner than I had expected—a week earlier. I remember you very well,' he added. 'How are you and your family?'

'As well as possible, sir, thank you,' said Wilson, pressing the hand which Sebastian had held out to him. 'Do I see a friend of yours, sir?' he added, looking at Hugo, who was watching the man with the preternatural solemnity which was one of his ways of showing that he was amused.

'Yes; a very great friend — Mr. Von Birkenau,' was all Sebastian said; and added: 'I want to go through the works. I asked that young fellow who was here, who——'

'I hope he wasn't rude, sir. I trust he didn't make himself unpleasant,' said Wilson fervently.

'Why, is he insubordinate usually, or rude to his superiors?' asked Sebastian, with a sudden keenness of look, in strong contrast with his soft voice and gentle manner.

'Insubordinate! no, sir. A better work-

man or an honester young fellow never lived ;
only he's got the idea that he hasn't got no
superiors—and it will bring him into trouble.
I often tell him so.'

'But he is clever and honest, you say ?'
said Sebastian, pausing to ask the question.

'Yes, sir,' said Wilson, who was fond of
Myles, and had been fond of him for years.
'He's got the brains of half a dozen of the
usual run, and you might trust him with un-
told gold ; ay, and more dangerous things
than that. But he is apt to give a little too
much of his sauce.'

'Ah ! Well, we will go on now, if you
please ; and when Mr. Sutcliffe comes in, I'll
get him to go on and lunch with me. I
should like to say a few words to the—
"hands," is it you call them ? if there is any
place where they could come to listen to
me.'

'Surely, sir ! The big yard will hold them
all, and more than them.'

'Then be good enough to lead the way,'

said Sebastian, looking at his watch suggestively.

Wilson was a proud and a happy man that
morning, as he led the newly-arrived lord of
that place through the maze of great rooms
and machinery, and pointed out all the im-
provements, the wonderful contrivances for
making wood and steel and iron do the work
of hands and feet; all the 'perfection of
mechanism, human and metallic,' of which
the factory and its contents formed an example.

Sebastian followed him : his eyes had lost
their sleepy look ; he asked many questions,
acute enough, for all the indifferent tone of
them.   He seemed to have much of the gift
which is said to be royal—the eye which
took in with incredible rapidity both details
and generalities.   Very little that was to be
seen escaped him, including the curious
glances and the loud comments and surmises
relative to himself.

It took an hour to go even quickly through

the different rooms, and then Wilson, saying, 'This is the last, sir, the warehouse,' took them into a large, well-lighted room, in which were some half-dozen men at work: Myles Heywood in the centre. Sebastian stooped to Hugo, whispering:

'I want to speak to that young fellow alone a few minutes.'

Hugo stepped up to a large pile of cloth, seemingly interested in some mystic marks and figures upon it, which he requested Wilson to explain; while Sebastian, going on, stopped at Myles's side, and looking at his work, said:

'That is cut-looking, is it?'

'Yes.'

'Well, I've learnt something. Listen to me a moment, will you?'

Myles looked up inquiringly.

'I am going to say something to all these people directly, and I want you to promise to come and listen to it; will you?'

Half vexed, half flattered, Myles looked

into Mallory's face. He had not given up his notion that the young man was a 'jackanapes;' but if so, the 'jackanapes' had a manner that it was not easy for even a superior person to resist. Myles replied:

' Certainly, I will come.'

He looked as if he were going to add something—in fact it was on the tip of his tongue to say : ' I don't promise to like what I shall hear ;' but he refrained. He remembered Adrienne, and his promise. Yet he had the conviction that he would dislike what Sebastian had to say. A Conservative— Southern sympathies, no doubt. What could such an one have to say that he would like ? But he would go, if only to watch till the cloven foot showed itself.

At that moment Wilson came up again.

' You've seen the last of the rooms, sir. If you're ready, I'll have the bell rung, and then we can go out into the yard.'

In a few minutes the great bell had clanged out, the engines had been stopped, the hands were streaming out into the yard.

Sebastian and Wilson stood upon a huge empty lurry that was close by one of the warehouse doors, so that they had nothing to do but step on to it, which they did, while Myles and his comrades swung themselves on to the ground, and took their stand in a knot, not far away from this impromptu platform.

Sebastian looked keenly at all the up-turned faces, while Wilson made a few brief, yet remarkably entangled and involved introductory remarks.

The overlooker's voice ceased. He swung himself from the lurry, and went and stood with the crowd.

'My friends,' began Sebastian, 'circumstances have kept me for ten years away from Lancashire. Perhaps I might still not have made the necessary effort to return, but for this great struggle which is going on in America, and whose direct effects will first be felt in Lancashire. When that began, I felt I had no right to remain any longer away. I have heard, and one or two little things which I have seen, even during the few hours I have been in Thanshope, lead me to feel that the saying is a true one, that you Lancashire men are inclined to despise an employer who does not know his business, much as you would despise a workman who did not know his work. The principle is a right and honest one; and I don't say that I may not have come under the head of those who deserve some contempt as being ignorant, and " absentee owners." Even since I came here, I have discovered that I never knew what work was before; I see that my task will be no easy one, to master the principles of my business, and to try and provide in some degree against the dark days which, I fear, are almost inevitable. But, hard or easy, it is a task I mean to learn. The time is coming, as I think all thoughtful men must see—

coming rapidly, when Lancashire will have to exert every effort to meet that distress which will rush upon her ; that cloud that is hastening across the Atlantic is a very black cloud, and will make the days very dark. Let us try manfully, hand in hand, to breast the storm together.

'I suppose that you all, or nearly all, will agree with me upon at least one point—sympathy with the Federal side in this struggle. (A murmur, deep and strong, of profound approbation arose—a murmur in which men's and women's voices alike joined.) 'That noble man, Abraham Lincoln, against whose honour the Southern press has lifted its impotent voice—not to mention some journals in this country, which Englishmen ought to be ashamed to read,—that noble man, should he live and be fortunate in his grand crusade, will benefit all the world by his intrepidity. He cannot give you cheap and abundant supplies of cotton now, but by his courage and wisdom he is securing your future supplies upon a firm basis, very different from the slippery vantage-ground of slave labour upon which they have hitherto depended.' (Another murmur indicative of that approval which, to their honour, Lancashire working men and women, throughout those bitter years, gave to the Federal side, greeted the speaker.)

'I understand that you Lancashire men, especially you Thanshope men, think a great deal of politics and principles. So you ought, considering who is your member, and that other great name which is connected with Thanshope. I also know that in spite of the strong Conservative element amongst your gentry, and, they tell me, amongst the workmen too' (a voice : 'Conservative workingman—there's no such thing !')—'in spite of this alleged Conservative element, you have always, since you first returned a representative to Parliament, returned a Radical.

'I was not aware of the strength of the feeling upon this point in Thanshope. I have always myself held politics to be secondary to some other subjects, but, since I find so much interest centred round the point here, and moreover, since persons whom I have met and spoken to have treated me on the tacit assumption that I was a Conservative, I judge it as well to tell you, face to face, that, whatever I may be on other matters, in politics I am no Conservative, but a Radical. Of course there are almost as many kinds of Radicals as there are of Dissenters. The details of my radicalism and those of your radicalism are, I dare say, somewhat different ; but I hope we shall both be able to respect the principle and never mind the form.

'Now I will not keep you longer—only let me say, finally, I am here to learn my business, and to try to guide my ship through the storm that is coming. Thanshope, as you know, is one of the places where the pinch of distress will be soonest felt, since the counts of yarns used here are precisely those, the supply of which will soonest fall off. I ask a promise from you, and I make one to you. In that time that is coming I ask you to trust me—my feelings and intentions towards you, and on my part I promise to strain every nerve to do my duty by you. We will work on as long as there is cotton to be had, and then—I trust, for your sakes, and mine, and that of humanity at large, that it will not be long that I shall have to help you in your fight to keep the wolf from the door.'

He stopped, bowed, and was turning away, when they gave him a hearty cheer; and one or two voices informed him laconically that they 'reckoned he was one o' th' reet sort,' and that 'he'd suit.'

He jumped down from the lurry, joined Wilson and his friend Hugo, and went with them towards the office. The engineer returned to his post; soon the busy machinery was in full roar again, as if there had been no such thing as war—no such parties as

Federals and Confederates. The interruption to the morning's work was already a thing of the past—an incident to be talked about.

Myles Heywood maintained entire silence upon the subject, nor could any one of all who inquired of him get him to say what he thought of the new master. He might have deep thoughts about it—at least they were unexpressed. The rest of the hands talked the event over with lively excitement. The general impression was a favourable one. The men liked what he had said, though he was generally pronounced to be 'a bit too much of a swell,' and it was agreed that he 'spoke rather fine,' and, they said, minced his words too much; was, in short, rather too much of a fine gentleman. Otherwise he was considered sound, and they were pleased to find him on the right side in politics.

The women, too, liked him, for reasons apparently similar to those alleged by Peter

van den Bosch, as their grounds for liking
Philip van Artevelde :

> 'And wenches who were there, said Artevelde
> Was a sweet name, and musical to hear.'

Mary Heywood, at least, said she 'liked the
chap : he had siccan a soft voice, and a nice,
smooth-soundin' name, like.'

The general conclusion was a very Lancashire one : that the young man had spoken
well and reasonably ; sensibly enough for a
person who knew nothing about his business,
but that 'fair words butter no parsnips ;' and
the conjecture may reasonably be hazarded
whether Sebastian's speech had induced any
one of his hearers to form a decided opinion,
good or bad, of him. They waited to see,
and indeed the time was striding forward
with fearful rapidity, nearer and nearer, when
the sincerity of his profession should be put
to the proof.

CHAPTER XIII.

INITIATION.

EBASTIAN and Hugo drove away from the factory, accompanied by Mr. Sutcliffe, the manager and head man of the business. Arrived at the Oakenrod, Mallory and his manager retired to the library, and there plunged straight into business.

Mr. Sutcliffe was a small, mild-looking man, with eyes that were keen despite his nervous, almost timid expression, a bald head, spectacles, a gentle smile, and a large bundle of what he called 'documents.'

Over these documents he and Sebastian

remained absorbed until luncheon was announced. They tarried not long over that meal. Hugo von Birkenau appeared to be a very familiar friend, for Sebastian made no excuse for leaving him, and with a slight apology to his mother, he and Mr. Sutcliffe returned to the library.

An hour, two, three hours passed, chiefly occupied in expositions from Mr. Sutcliffe on the nature of the business, its principles, and the method of carrying it on. Sebastian's part consisted chiefly in listening, naturally ; but every now and then he interposed with a question—questions so much to the point, and showing such discernment and discrimination, that Mr. Sutcliffe, who had at first begun his task with some constraint and great dryness of manner and tone, brightened visibly every minute ; his tone grew warmer, his manner more animated, his eyes flashed now and then. Thus the interview went on, until Mr. Sutcliffe, laying down a bundle of papers, whose import he had just explained, took up another bundle, and was beginning,

'These refer to the——'

But Sebastian interrupted him.

'Excuse me, Mr. Sutcliffe. Suppose we lay aside business for to-day. I want to ask you some other questions. With such a manager as you, I have no fear of things going wrong.'

Mr. Sutcliffe smiled.

'Judging from what I have heard and seen of you, Mr. Mallory, you will soon be in a position to manage your own business. You must not feel offended when I say that I have been most agreeably disappointed—surprised is perhaps rather the word.'

Sebastian smiled a little.

'I am a fearfully indolent fellow, I believe,' said he. 'I take a lot of rousing; but once set me to plod at a thing, and I continue until I understand it — at least, I think so.'

'That is a very modest way of describing

your ready comprehension of details which must be as strange to you as those we have just been discussing. But that's neither here nor there ; you wanted some other information ?'

' I suppose you are pretty well acquainted with the different parties, social and political, in the town, and with the characters, at any rate, of the leading people ?'

' I may say that I certainly am.'

' Well, to begin with, I wish you would tell me candidly what character is borne by my own concern and the management of it ?'

Mr. Sutcliffe looked up quickly, an almost startled expression upon his face.

' That is rather a delicate matter,' he began.

' Yes, I suppose it is. But I am sure you will be frank with me. I drew my own conclusions from what I saw and heard this morning, and I want to find out if your account agrees with them. Never mind how disagreeable it may be.'

'Your works, then, bear a very high reputation in many respects. Your hands are as decent and as steady a lot as any in the town, take them all in all. Things are generally peaceable. It is looked upon, and with justice, as an increasing, thoroughly prosperous concern. Our goods, both yarns and cloth, have got a name. I like the men who are under me, and I think they like me —Wilson, and Heywood, and the others. I think I have succeeded in keeping things right; but——'

'Well?'

'There are some misunderstandings about yourself—some prejudices. They don't like absentee owners here, and that's a fact. But I'm sure that impression will soon be effaced, now that you are here yourself. If you show them that you don't mean play——'

Sebastian shrugged his shoulders.

'*Mon Dieu!* There does not seem to be much question of play. I never saw anything so oppressively in earnest as every one here seems to be. It is stamped upon almost every face you meet. Certainly I am not in play.'

'Then they will soon find that out, and respect you accordingly.'

'But that is not all you were going to say?'

'It may seem a small kind of complaint to make; but it's better to let you know the truth at once. There certainly is a feeling against Mrs. Mallory.'

Sebastian looked up in surprise.

'Against my mother? What has she to do with it?'

'A feeling that she is not sufficiently liberal in her ideas, and that she would, if she could get the authority, interfere unduly in matters which, with the utmost respect to her, she does not understand, never having had occasion to study them. I am bound to say that, though I have never had anything like a dispute with Mrs. Mallory, yet that is my own impression too, and that is one reason why I rejoice at your return. You are now the final authority.'

The murder was out, and Mr. Sutcliffe's shrewd eyes watched the young man's face attentively. He did not look angry, did not look even annoyed; but rather thoughtful for a moment. Then he said:

'I am glad you mentioned it. Of course, that is not a topic for discussion. As you said, my presence will make all the difference. Is that all about my own works?'

'Yes. I don't think there is anything else.'

'Who are the leading men here?'

'So far as money goes, there are a good many big men here. Mr. Spenceley is reported to be the richest, and I believe report is right.'

'Spenceley! Ah! What about him?'

'He is a spinner; does an enormous trade. They say he has been speculating rather too much lately. He has a certain influence in some quarters, but it is an influence that will die with him.'

' How so ?'

' He has only a son and a daughter, and
the son is probably the biggest blackguard in
the place ; he will never have any influence.
The daughter, I hear, is rather an eccentric
young lady.'

' Oh !' was all Sebastian said.

Mr. Sutcliffe went on :

' The son, I believe, is a very black sheep.
It was only a week or two ago that he insulted some young woman—in a small place,
you see, these things make a good deal of
noise—in a most abominable manner ; but he
was punished for that, for the girl's sweetheart—at least that is one of the tales, I
don't believe it myself ; but one thing is quite
certain, a young working-man followed him
to his club that very night, and gave him a
good hiding in the billiard-room. No one, I
don't think one soul, was sorry for him. The
feeling was so dead against him that he did
not even prosecute.'

' I have heard some account of it. But

don't you know who the young man was who did it ?'

Mr. Sutcliffe smiled a little as he said :

' In my own mind, I believe I could lay my finger upon the man ; but as I thoroughly respect him for what he did, and should be sorry to get him into trouble, I shall keep quiet about it.'

Sebastian looked inquiringly at him.

' I believe the man was one of your own workpeople—Heywood, a fellow I have known from the time when he first came as a half-timer.'

' I have seen the man. You think it was he. Why ?'

' Partly because I was passing the club-door at the very time of the row, and saw him come out of it, looking rather dangerous, with a couple of straps in his hand ; and, secondly, because when it has been discussed, which you will easily believe has been pretty actively, he has looked embarrassed, and kept perfect silence upon the subject.'

Sebastian nodded.

'Miss Spenceley is a great friend of Mrs. Mallory,' went on the manager. 'But that's neither here nor there; only they are about the biggest people, in a money point of view, in the place. There are several other families something like them. Then there's Canon Ponsonby, the radical parson, our vicar, a very fine old gentleman; you will like him. He is respected by all who are themselves worthy of respect, be they churchmen or dissenters.'

'Naturally the feeling here is radical?'

'Tremendous; and North, almost to a man. Lots of these working-men know what's coming; and it *is* coming upon them too, like the very devil. They'll tell you they know the cotton must run out soon, or run up to such a price that we can hardly get it. But if they have to do without it, or with Surats——'

'What on earth is " Surats " ?'

'Indian cotton; abominable stuff to work.

Haven't you—but of course you haven't—
heard of the weaver who put up the prayer,
" O Lord ! send us cotton ; *but not Surats !*"
But if they have to work Surats, they'll stick
to it that North is right, and South wrong ;
and they'll clem rather than have anything to
say to Jeff Davis.'

' How soon do you think distress will
begin ?'

' I think we shall have to shut up shop by
Christmas.   It's of no use talking much about
it beforehand.   All I can say is, there's a
time coming which will prove Lancashire
once for all, her rich and her poor alike ; and
show them up to the world in a light as fierce
as that of the midday sun.   We shall get to
see the stuff we're made of.   And there's
half-past five ; I must go.'

' Won't you stay and dine with us ?'

' I have another engagement, thank you.
To-morrow, at the same time, Mr. Mallory,
we will resume the discussion, if you feel so
inclined.'

'Certainly. I shall expect you. Good-evening.'

He was left, leaning against the mantel-piece, to reflect upon what had passed.

A tap at the door was followed by the entrance of his mother.

'Have you finished at last, Sebastian? I have had no opportunity to tell you that I am expecting a friend to dine with us to-night.'

'Oh, are you? Who may he be?'

'She is Helena Spenceley, a very great favourite of mine. If my son will spend all his time away from home, I am obliged to find some kind of a substitute, you know. She has been almost like a daughter to me.'

'Any relative of the young man who recently distinguished himself by earning a thrashing?'

Mrs. Mallory looked annoyed.

'He is her brother,' said she coldly. 'He is away from home now. You must not judge Helena by him. Poor girl! She has a sad, unhappy home. I believe I really have been a friend to her. And I like to see young people about me.'

'Yes, of course.'

'I hope you have no engagement?'

'None at all. I shall be delighted to make Miss Spenceley's acquaintance.'

She retired, after casting a comprehensive glance around at the papers which strewed the table.

END OF VOL. I.

BILLING AND SONS, PRINTERS, GUILDFORD, SURREY.

S. & H.

www.ingramcontent.com/pod-product-compliance
Lightning Source LLC
Chambersburg PA
CBHW031333070726
47496CB00018B/1846